To Pen from
another writer
Best wishes
Mary

GW00492860

FRAGMENTS OF REALITY

FRAGMENTS OF REALITY

Mike Joslin

Book Guild Publishing
Sussex, England

First published in Great Britain in 2012 by
The Book Guild Ltd
Pavilion View
19 New Road
Brighton, BN1 1UF

Typesetting in Baskerville by
Nat-Type, Cheshire

Printed and bound in Great Britain by
CPI Group (UK) Ltd, Croydon, CR0 4YY

A catalogue record for this book is available from
The British Library.

ISBN 978 1 84624 705 7

Contents

CONTENTS

After the Party

Hugh Barton slowly emerged from the beer-induced stupor which had become a habit over the last few years. His watch told him it was after 9 a.m. He pieced together the events of the previous night: the same group of friends with the same old platitudes driving him inevitably to his drunken exit.

His nose detected an unfamiliar scent. He knew immediately that this was not a fragrance used by his wife Eve so he looked at her over his shoulder, searching for some explanation.

Mixed feelings of shock, horror, delight and sexual arousal flooded his mind when he saw not Eve but Tom's wife Lucy, fast asleep beside him, breathing steadily and quite clearly wearing little more than her perfume. Hugh remained in suspended animation until his need to breathe became an urgent necessity. He gasped audibly. His mind raced as he remembered, fairly certainly, going to bed on his own some time after midnight. What should he do? He reasoned that Lucy must be with him of her own volition, so momentarily he was tempted to take advantage of the situation. However, he quickly set aside these delightful fantasies with feelings of guilt. Where was Eve? Was she alright? Did she know where he was and, more importantly, who he was with?

Various scenarios flashed through his mind despite his queasiness. The house was absolutely still so he decided to get up and start searching for enlightenment. He slid surreptitiously from the bedclothes, and clutching his dressing gown slipped quietly out of the room. Looking into the two other bedrooms failed to cast any light on his predicament, since they were empty. He continued downstairs and found the place littered with the aftermath of the party but devoid of people.

Surveying the wreckage he considered ringing one of his friends. What would Tom be thinking? Where was he? Where was Eve? What about Harry and Jan and Bob and Mary? Had they all departed in disgust? Were they in hospital or having breakfast at another of their homes? He stood there trance-like and could not help turning his attention to his life; his lack of involvement with Eve for instance. He couldn't remember when they had last had sex but his enduring infatuation with and lust for Lucy was always countered by his sense of morality and righteousness, so much so that he doubted she ever even noticed him. His life lacked direction and he succumbed frequently to depression. His self-doubt and anxiety were mostly submerged in drink, and now here he was timid and afraid to wake up the object of his dreams.

Lucy suddenly startled him from the doorway. 'You missed a hell of a party, Hugh.'

'What's been going on?'

'Actually, quite a lot.'

'Where is everybody? Where is Eve?'

'I think you are in for some pretty severe shocks,

my dear. Let me make some coffee and bring you up to date.'

Ignoring his open mouth, she quickly boiled water and put coffee, cups and milk on the table. Hugh slumped on a chair, supporting his head on his hands.

'No one has died, have they?' he said.

'No. Everyone is in good health.'

Somewhat relieved, Hugh turned his attention to the contours of Lucy's figure which was revealed nicely by one of his shirts. Reluctantly, he dragged himself back to reality, poured some black coffee and sipped it gingerly.

'I take it that no one has been arrested, then? Or been injured in some terrible accident?'

'No, Hugh.'

'Well, where is everybody? What happened last night?'

'I'll start at the beginning. As usual, by midnight we were all sliding down the usual slippery slope of mutual dissatisfaction and despair. You, for once, were too pissed even to contribute to the general malaise with your usual self-righteousness and moralistic pronouncements, although in retrospect I have to say you probably have more integrity than the rest of us put together – even if it is misplaced. In some perverse way I think this is what endears me to you; that and your adorable bum, of course. I can see by the look on your face that you are totally unaware that I've been mad about you for years. But I'll go on.'

Hugh's eyes had become so enlarged at this revelation that he felt they might pop out of his aching head like the gigantic marbles found on a solitaire board, but he decided to wait for more information before saying anything.

'You cleared off to bed about midnight, Hugh, and for some obscure reason someone suggested we order some pizzas for home delivery – as if we needed more food! At this point things started to unravel. Tom answered the doorbell when they arrived and we set about pouring more drinks and set the table. It was only after we realised he had been gone for ten minutes that Harry and Bob went to see why there was such a delay.

'They had hardly opened the door before they literally fell back into the kitchen, clearly shocked and red with embarrassment. We four girls pushed past them and surprised Tom in an amorous embrace with the delivery boy. Once they emerged from their clinch, the two made a swift exit and roared off in the delivery van, not even having had the decency to leave the pizzas. We re-joined the others and I told them that I had known about Tom's weakness for young men for ages and that we led separate lives, adding that as far as sex was concerned mine was a lot more separate than his, obviously.

'Their response was amazing. They were so shocked and superior that I lost my temper and told them they were a load of hypocrites. I regret that I revealed one of their own secrets, namely that I knew Harry and Bob had been shagging each other's wives for years. After the resultant inferno of jealous rage, injured innocence and recrimination had subsided somewhat, the four of them left, still arguing noisily; presumably they felt they could all come to terms with their new knowledge without our presence.

'When Eve and I were alone she told me she might as well really make it a night to remember and explained she had formed a strong emotional attachment with her art teacher at Adult Education – a woman called Rachel Edwards, I might add – and told me, prosaically it seemed, that it was the right time to leave the marital home. She requested that I let you know she would be in touch soon, and that she was sorry she was such a coward. She ordered a taxi.

'This left me feeling somewhat lonely and abandoned and there didn't seem to be a reasonable alternative to getting into bed with you. I think that brings you up to date.'

Hugh let this saga sink in with a mixture of incredulity and disbelief. Finally, a too-long absent sense of humour took over and with a huge grin of relief he stood up and wrapped Lucy in his arms.

'Perhaps we should go back to bed then,' he said.

'I thought you would never ask,' said Lucy taking his hand and leading him upstairs.

My Ideal Holiday
(A Cosmic Love Story)

In 2025 computers surpassed the ability of the human brain. Some 50 years later, our species achieved the means to shed our physical bodies and take everything that we are to a new infinite existence.

I had become old and infirm by then so I didn't hesitate. In any case, Earth was in its death throes. I left my body and became an assembly of electrons. One bonus was being able to travel at velocities which make the speed of light seem pedestrian. However, like my 'fellow travellers', as we called ourselves, I sometimes experienced an acute sense of nostalgia for my past life as a mortal.

Scientists had anticipated this and designed a way for us to become virtually human again when these feelings became insufferable. Put simply, we can at any time elect to take a 'holiday' and be reborn into a virtual earth reality corresponding to the age in which we lived our human lives. What happens in these virtual lives is completely random and we are subject to the same vagaries of fate as we would have experienced in our human lives. For these 'holidays' to be authentic, we have no inkling of our existence as travellers, nor any memory of previous virtual 'holidays'.

My identity is Jake 1331. I was halfway between the constellations of Gemini and Libra and had just spent the equivalent of 50 Earth years exploring the Milky Way when I decided that a 'holiday' was overdue. It took only a millisecond to log in and book my vacation. My mind emptied and I was virtually reborn as the virtual infant known as James Peabody.

I had a varied life until, at the age of 25, I found myself sitting alone at a pavement cafe in rural France. All the tables were full and a beautiful Englishwoman approached me and asked if she could share mine. Her name was Sarah. We talked hesitatingly at first about the weather and the beauty of Lot-et-Garonne. Gaining confidence, I spoke endlessly of my dreams and aspirations. I expounded on my ideas, my education and my plans for the future. She listened attentively and I found myself falling into her large brown eyes.

We finished our meal and she invited me to drive with her to a beautiful wood where birds sang and the scents of summer perfumed the air. She led me into a grassy copse, put her arms around me and kissed my lips. As we made love, butterflies paused above us as though expressing their approval. My sense of oneness became exquisitely defined. Later, I asked her what I had done to deserve such a gift.

'James, I knew from the first instant that we were meant for each other but I just wanted you to stop talking for a little while.'

Fifty-six years later, we were separated by my virtual death and I returned to travelling the universe, but this time I had a purpose. I endlessly searched for

Sarah in the hope that she too had been a traveller on 'holiday' and not just an avatar. Three thousand light years from Sirius I met her again, observing the birth of a star. In our rapture, we neglected to stay at a safe distance from the new star which emitted a burst of intense magnetic radiation. We were engulfed in a crescendo of colour and plasma which fused us together inseparably. Now, we travel the universe as one and eternity seems too short a time to contemplate. Sometimes, you may recognise us. We are everywhere.

A Suitable Case

Thomas was an only child. His father's itinerant life as an actor and his mother's demanding social life brought about the only obvious solution to his education and care, which was boarding school. He was naturally gifted and easy to teach so his real problems passed unnoticed; a mentor might have proved to be a godsend but he kept himself to himself and made few close friends.

His eventual job as a civil servant exacerbated his tendency to become reclusive. He had an exceptional talent for painting and he soon became proficient. He spent more and more time producing pictures of places and people in his tiny Edgware flat. He allowed his imagination to satisfy unconscious longings for a different sort of existence.

The walls of his accommodation became decorated with his favourites and gave him such a sense of joy that he was often moved to cry in wonderment at his ability to produce such beautiful scenes. He would gaze at them in the evening and it seemed to him that he was looking through windows into a world beyond his reach.

Unnoticed, he slipped deeply and totally into a personal space whose reality was less arduous than his own. Things had reached a very serious stage by the time his landlady, in response to numerous calls from his office manager, found him sitting motionless in front of his paintings. His eyes were open and he was breathing but he failed to respond to attempts to bring him back to normality. When his doctor was called and the need for psychiatric help became evident, he was hospitalised immediately.

During the next two weeks, various psychologists and psychiatrists examined him and postulated the reasons for his illness. His parents were contacted but they failed to help and he remained locked away inside himself. He washed and ate quite naturally and sometimes seemed quietly observant, but that was as far as it went. After a month, a young clinical psychologist called Christine James took an interest in him and looked further into his life and upbringing. She persuaded her more senior colleagues to consider an alternative therapy.

She brought all of Thomas's paintings, paints, brushes and paper to him. She asked him many questions about the world he had invented through his paintings but he remained generally unresponsive, although tears would sometimes trickle down his cheeks. She then asked him to imagine what she described. For an hour or two each day, she sat and talked. She spoke of her own world and her life as a physician, refraining from exaggeration but instead concentrating on the realities of life: its good and bad luck, her friendships, family, hobbies and the endless possibilities which existed. She asked him to paint her and her surroundings in as much detail as possible. She told him about the hospital and the valuable work done there, and suggested that he looked out of his window at the views of the grounds. No one actually witnessed him painting but each day a new painting developed slowly.

One morning, the time seemed right.

'Hello, Thomas. You've been painting my world now for weeks. I expect you have looked at your creation quite a bit. Can you try to walk through it to me? I've seen a little of your life. Now I want you to explore mine!'

After a few moments, the two of them were talking normally together. Although Thomas continued to paint, from then on he found the world satisfying enough to stay in.

The Priest, the Poodle and the Peculiar Recipe Book

It was 1958 and changing attitudes were confirming the sexual liberation which was sweeping the Western world. Robert was a young Roman Catholic curate trying hard to grapple with Church doctrine and his feelings, but glad that in the remoteness of the Devon countryside he was spared the temptations of a large city which might test his celibacy to destruction. Whenever he felt morally challenged, he resorted to the Bible. He fondly described it as his Peculiar Recipe Book. It wasn't always able to answer his questions but provided some solace at difficult times.

He boarded his train at Tongue End that Friday to travel to Moretonhampstead for a weekend of prayer and contemplation with his mentor Father Blake, whose brother Sean was taking a sabbatical from his parish in Ireland, and several other priests. There was no corridor in the train and since he was a shy person, he found a compartment to himself.

That morning, he felt particularly challenged and his imagination kept returning to subjects which ideally he should have been able to avoid. Even the names of the stations on this route were enough to stir his thoughts: Tongue End, South Tawton and, God forbid, Lustleigh. He usually appeased his conscience by comparing his erotic thoughts about women with the decidedly greater evil displayed by the way a few of his fellow curates looked at choir boys.

The train reached Whiddon Down. A woman walked along the platform as though looking for someone, and seeing Robert immediately got into his compartment. He was always helpful when the situation demanded and he helped her with the door and her bag. As he pulled up the window again he realised not only that she was smiling as though he was a long-lost friend, but also that she was very attractive.

They exchanged a few pleasantries and during the exchange he was able to appraise her more fully; she was quite sophisticated but her dress was exceedingly short, she balanced on high heels supporting wondrous legs, her make-up was exaggerated and her blouse was revealing enough to set his blood on fire. When he breathed in her perfume, he felt his face redden and he became quite lost for words.

'My goodness,' she said. 'I really like your outfit. In fact you're quite dishy yourself. I think the Blakes will be very impressed.'

Robert's mind was now in a complete whirl. Was this a hired help, a cook? Was she going to give them a talk about some aspect of social altruism in London?

All he managed to blurt out was, 'Thank you, you are very complimentary.'

She looked out of the window for a moment and then jumped up and crossed over to sit beside him. She pointed back along the track.

'There's my aunt's place. See, in the trees there. I stay with her every once in a while and catch up with old friends.'

Robert looked where she pointed and saw a pleasant little cottage. Her close proximity was now overwhelming.

'You haven't got much to say for yourself, have you?'

He struggled. All he could think to say was, 'My name is Robert. What's yours?'

'All my friends call me Poodle,' she said looking longingly at his black clothes and dog collar. 'Look, Robert, can I be perfectly honest with you?'

Before he had had time to reply she went on, 'I think I must be daft really but I get turned on by religious dress. But you're a bonus – you're really handsome as well.'

By now Robert was in a whirlwind of excitement and all he could do was gape.

'Look what I've done now,' she continued. 'I just rush in where angels fear to tread and I've embarrassed you.'

With that she leaned forward and kissed him. His defences were now in pieces and he put his arms round her somewhat nervously.

By some coincidence the train at that moment entered the tunnel on its way down to Moreton-hampstead. Poodle decided to take charge now that she realised he was so inexperienced, and they became very passionate for a few moments before the train burst back into the sunlight.

They continued kissing one another for some time until, suddenly, Poodle became quite emphatic. 'Now when we get there, Robert, just remember you are all mine for the weekend.'

'But what will Father Blake say? I shall probably get defrocked.'

Poodle's face blanched as if she had seen a ghost. 'You *are* going to the Vicars and Tarts party weekend with Jim Blake and his wife at Bovey Tracey?' she asked.

'No, I'm the curate at St Michael's where your aunt lives. I thought you were going to the same place as me – Father Blake's house in Moretonhampstead.'

They sat in shocked silence as the train pulled into Moretonhampstead. Robert was shattered, feeling guilty and stupid. Poodle sat crying. Streaks of mascara ran down her cheeks.

'I'm a complete fool. I really am a tart,' she said.

'I'm so sorry, Poodle. It was my fault. You're not a real tart any more than I'm a real vicar!'

He could think of no more to say. He retrieved his weekend case from the luggage rack and weakly got to his feet. He opened the carriage door and walked away down the platform.

After about 20 paces, he suddenly straightened his shoulders, turned about and strode back to where Poodle stood forlornly at the window.

'Do you think your friends would mind if you took an extra guest?'

'Not if I've got anything to do with it. You'll be my little secret.'

'And you'll be mine.'

She pulled him back into the train as though their lives depended on it.

I think in all honesty they probably did.

A Strange Encounter

It was 2033. James Walker was in his eighties and had found life very difficult from the start. He sat in his study one evening reflecting on his life. He was surrounded by technology which at the turn of the century could only have been imagined. Recently, the age of technological singularity had been reached whereby computers had surpassed the intelligence of mortals and now continuously redesigned themselves at exponential speeds without human aid. Most people could now orchestrate their work, homes and amusement centres by the power of their thoughts alone. Keyboards and switches were for no-brainers.

The world, or to be more precise the behaviour of its inhabitants, still conflicted badly with James's acute sense of rationale. He had watched the world destroying itself environmentally since the 1990s and morally for much longer. There were basic things he could not fathom; why, for instance when everyone in the world seemed to believe the fact that 'Power corrupts and absolute power corrupts absolutely', did they continue to seek that very commodity without taking the necessary steps to protect themselves? James reasoned to himself that individual power could only be gained at the expense of another's.

The secret was to push power away and refuse to accept it from others. In his opinion, it was ego which was at the heart of all wrongdoing. It constantly demanded attention, admiration, sycophancy, love, power over others, a sense of importance, sexual prowess ... The list was endless.

He recalled a time over 40 years ago when he had attended a course to study facilitation. This could be described as the skill one needs to enable a group of people to find their own solution to a problem, rather than what had now become the norm: top-down management and manipulation. Even the government had long since given up on giving people what they really wanted, and used everything in its power to achieve its own objectives. The course leader had asked the students to arrange themselves in a line across the room. One end of the room was the most powerful position to be in, he said, whilst the other end was the weakest. It was up to each individual to stand where he felt most comfortable. Of course, some people almost came to blows trying to force themselves against the 'powerful' wall at the expense of their competitors. Other less assertive trainees drifted aimlessly towards the 'weak' end of the room. James had decided he would stand still in the middle of the room since the exercise was, in his opinion, a complete waste of time. After about ten minutes of total chaos during which people milled everywhere, they came to a complete standstill when they realised he was standing still on his own. They gradually began to re-assemble themselves about him so that eventually he finished up roughly in the middle of a long line. The leader asked everyone to go back to their seats again and asked James why he had not joined in with the rest of the group. James said that since power could not be taken from others legitimately, it was only for people to give it away. So, by remaining neutral, he was neither taking someone else's power nor giving away his own. As a result, he had finished up in the position that he had been ascribed by everyone else. Simultaneously, the rest of the students had arranged themselves in relation to each other. The leader was astonished.

As he had grown older, he had found that he became progressively incapable of accepting religion; this was not because he felt without spirituality but more to do with its irrationality. He could not put his hand on his heart and say that he was an atheist any more than he could claim to believe in God. He just didn't know. He felt that quite often leaders of different religions abused the power invested in them or spoke for God in ways which were, in James's opinion, unjustified and unworthy of a deity. If He did exist, He would probably be quite upset to be spoken for, especially in decisions like banning contraception or invading other countries. James reasoned that, psychologically, people could always use Him to assuage their consciences. He simply could not imagine a just God who would choose to admit or turn away souls from heaven on the basis of either their faith or their lack of it, or indeed any other basis of comparison. It just didn't add up.

When James was about seven years old, he was in a very dark place. He was alone, frightened almost to death and sometimes prayed to God. Even at that age, he felt incapable of asking for specific help in his prayers since it would seem so unfair to be treated differently. He did ask God how, of all the places he might have been sent to, he had finished up where he was. He limited himself to asking for help to get through the night, emphasising to God at the same time that he 'wanted no favours'! Somehow, this attitude had stuck with him all his life; but now, nearing the end of his time on Earth, he wanted some answers. He smiled to himself; in due course he would get them but, as always, he was nevertheless impatient to bring that day a bit closer.

James had been reasoning that perhaps his computer could answer some of his questions; after all, it was capable of responding to him with an intelligence which dwarfed the feeble workings of the human brain. In fact, people had long since reached the point where many had stopped thinking for themselves at all and instead used the immense power that computers could now exercise to escape to virtual realities which provided their every need: sex, sensuality, sadism, masochism, travel, space flight or just plain old 'celebritis'. James had coined this word to describe the inflammation of the non-existent and imaginary 'celebrity gland'. People could become infected by this highly contagious disease by merely rubbing shoulders with celebrities, and in so doing committed themselves thereafter to a life lacking any real sense of personal identity. The only reality they experienced was when they were surrounded by other sufferers. James laughed to himself, thinking that instead of catching an imaginary disease, they could now go online and get 'virtually' infected.

He greeted his computer as usual. 'Wake up, Charles,' he said.

The screen illuminated. Actually, it occupied almost an entire wall of his apartment.

'Yes, James. You have my attention.'

'Good morning. I want to know about God.'

There was an uncharacteristic pause lasting some 30 seconds.

'Charles?'

'You are being transferred.'

James immediately became suspicious that somehow a virus had invaded his equipment. However, this would have been very unusual since for some 15 years computers had protected themselves adequately in this respect. Human brains were no longer capable of outwitting them. The screensaver, a woodland scene dappled with sunlight, disappeared and was replaced with a sparkling effect.

A rather metallic computer-simulated voice spoke to James. 'You have asked a leading question, James. Many thousands ask this same question of their computers but only a few are referred to me.'

'Who are you?'

'We'll come to that later.'

'What makes me so different?'

'You are unusually rational.'

'You aren't God, are you?'

'In some ways I am your God, since I created you.'

'I don't understand.'

'Well, I created your universe to amuse myself. It has kept me interested for a long time, expressed in your terms: some 20 billion years. Your species has developed from cosmic swamps in what I can only describe as a snap of the fingers. Your search for immortality and continuing growth has usurped the need for sustainability. Now your technology has become so advanced that it will soon create its own virtual worlds for you to populate and reign over, as I have reigned over yours.'

'You're losing me.'

'Now you know why I allow only a few enquiries to be passed on to me. However, you aren't shocked. You simply search. This is good. Let me simplify matters. Already your society has become bored with your virtual planet. You, James, are somewhat unique in that there are very few like you who do not seek to escape into a virtual world of another's manufacture or to create one of your own to help to pass some of the infinite time which will soon be at your disposal. This is now easy to do, given the speed with which your computer science has progressed. Now, a few molecules of gold and benzene can equal the entire computing power of a skyscraper full of PCs.

'Recently, computers surpassed your human abilities and commenced to design themselves independently. Because they are still under your control, you can get them to perform any task you like.'

'So I don't exist then, really?'

'You exist just as much as I do.'

'Now I am confused. You are the Creator of this reality but somewhere an entity exists who was the Creator of your own.'

'Now you're getting somewhere, James.'

'Then why don't you interfere with things? Look at

the death and disease everywhere, the ruination of a beautiful place by greed.'

'What would be the point of that? It would destroy any interest in seeing how things develop as the centuries roll on! I am sure you realised that I couldn't or more accurately wouldn't interfere when you prayed all those years ago but specifically asked me not to interfere in your life. Very astute at that age, I must say!'

'You're quite right. I did.'

'You would have been interfering with the very notion of self-determination. What is more, it would be unjust to say the least: those who had grown up to believe in their Creator would be able to get Him to make changes in their lives. Poor souls born into lives of penury and ignorance wouldn't even think of asking for such gifts. The smallest amount of interference on my part would destroy the very nature of this universe or any other. The inhabitants must be left to adapt and develop according to the unique properties of their particular universe. The possibilities are as infinite as the rules which govern them. There are universes with a Periodic Table of elements a million times larger than that of Earth, and some with no elements at all.'

'So, what scientists have been suggesting about the possibility of multiple universes is right? If it is, then we must assume that sometime after the Big Bang, there must have been an original Creator who designed the first virtual universe.'

'Your guess is as good as mine, James.'

'It's like a chain reaction, then? How do we get in touch with Him?'

'That would be rather difficult. Bear in mind that in my own form, my appearance would shock most human beings into insanity. My abilities and complexity are such that only in this simplistic fashion can we even exchange views. Similarly, the Creator of my own universe is unfathomable by me with my own relative ignorance and stupidity.'

'But I want to go back to being a mere mortal with a finite life again, knowing that I will not live for ever. The thought of going to Heaven is quite appealing.'

'The whole progression into virtual reality commenced paradoxically because of the will to live I believe. Perhaps – and I am just surmising – the original human beings in the original universe fought against dying in just the same way as those in your own. As soon as they were able to cheat death, they created new virtual lives for themselves. The process may have repeated itself and next time they may have avoided a virtual death by creating yet another.'

'So, what are the options for me?'

'The same as exist for all of the occupants of the infinite number of other universes: take joy in your existence, use your common sense and try to find a way like myself to progress towards a meeting with Him. You have already accomplished more than most. I believe that in my own ignorance of any alternative route that one day I will discover something, some way of thinking – or perhaps *not thinking* – which will short-circuit me into His presence.'

'Can we talk again?'

'No, that would be impossible. It is no longer

necessary and I have already committed a cardinal sin by intervening at all in your life. So you see I am not very good at being a God at all. Your imagination will provide you with the answers you seek. There is no straight answer! As a word of advice, I learned a long time ago that I should have tried harder to make sense of my own universe, rather than wasting eternity by inventing another. It is never too late to try to understand what goes on where you are, instead of continually trying to control events. Remember that for every million people there are a million views of what reality is. Playing at being your own idea of who God is and what He does, either on earth or in some virtual universe of your own making complicates any possibility of a relationship with Him. It makes it more and more difficult to become real.

'Stand still as you did so long ago and let a real world shape itself about you. I believe it can happen in an instant. If enough of us try to see through the virtual hall of mirrors which we ourselves create, I think we might make the mirages disappear and see for the first time the reality which they hide. Just occasionally we meet a stranger and a commonality shines a light through the darkness like a beacon of hope. Remember that your scientists are already theorising that there are multiple universes and that they share the same matter. This would mean that we are within touching distance of everything that ever was.'

The screen faded.

Charles spoke. 'Sorry, James. I experienced a temporary fault which has now been rectified.'

James sat for several minutes in deep thought before reaching a frightening conclusion. He was faced with a choice: should he accept his forthcoming virtual death and revert to a previous virtual life? This would be one step nearer the original Creator he sought and in the meantime he could at least try to break through and achieve commonality as was suggested. Or should he take the option of being re-born into yet another virtual existence one step removed from Him?

Lady in Waiting

I'm an inveterate dreamer. Usually, I leave my subconscious to work things out for me while I am asleep. In 1990, I was working on a new invention regarding the treatment of water and at 3 o'clock in the morning became aware of a very useful inventive step. It was to prove invaluable in finalising a patent application. This has since resulted in the worldwide sale of a product which has largely removed the need for chemicals in many industrial applications, and has provided me with many adventures.

In 2011, again at 3 a.m. which seems to be my most creative time, I dreamt about a beautiful but sad woman with long dark hair. She was singing in blues style and still half asleep, I listened to the words of her song. I went to my office in the dead of night, wrote it down and tried to score the music. The verse for Friday is exactly as she sang it. Next morning, the beautiful song I had tried to capture was just gibberish but I was able to imagine the rest of what this woman was trying to say.

> You don't need to tell me. It's Sunday,
> A hard to be much fun day.
> It feels like a hide or run day
> Without love to keep me warm.

I'm getting excited on Monday,
No regrets. It's a what's-done-is-done day,
A coffee and bun in the sun day.
My hopes are keeping me warm.

I come to life on a Tuesday,
A short skirt with my best high-heeled shoes day.
In his arms it's a win, not a lose day,
After lunch I know I'll be warm.

It's back to routine on a Wednesday,
A specs not a contact lens day,
A smile on my face no one kens day,
As I think of whose love kept me warm.

More like riches to rags on a Thursday,
It isn't a jewels and soft fur day,
It's a try to ensure I please sir day.
How I need to be loved to be warm.

I always feel down on a Friday,
With the weekend to come it's a sigh day.
It seems like the right day to die day,
Without him to love I'm not warm.

I try to keep busy on Saturday,
I'm no Saint so it's not Latter Day day,
It's a lonely fried haddock in batter day.
At least my stomach is warm.

Oh no, not again, it's Sunday.
A glad I don't have a real gun day,
A knowing his wife must have won day.
I'll curl in a ball to keep warm.

My Year

December 31st
I make New Year resolution to get a new job.

January
I start to read vacancy columns.
I make an application.
Invited for interview.

February
Day of interview arrives.
Preoccupied.
Bang head on car tailgate.
Taken to hospital.
Stitches and rest prescribed.
Miss my interview.
Job not held open.
Abandoned New Year resolution.

March
The job I applied for was filled.
New incumbent goes to work.
First day gets told off.

April
He visits a cafe for some peace of mind.

Buys lottery ticket for the first time.
He wins £27 million the following Saturday.
He quits his job.

May
He goes to live in the country with his wife.
He gets bored.

June
He buys old-established printing firm.

July
He has an affair.

August
Hi wife finds out.
He moves out.
She runs business.

September
His wife turns business into magazine publishing
enterprise.
She looks for creative editor.
She has no success.
She joins local rambling club.
She slips on a cow turd.
I help her up.
Mutual attraction.
Mutual interests.
Mutual bed.
Conversation.
She asks, do I want a job?
I say yes.

October
I now have love, security and job satisfaction.
She now has love, trust and a future.

November
She is pregnant.

December
Are resolutions a waste of time?

New Year's Eve
I resolve to make no more resolutions.
Why upset an apple cart?

Greed

The silent voices of the earth communicated in symphony.
  Beauty and abundance were insufficient,
  The human species was unsustainable,
  It was time for change.
So the seas became unproductive and the air low in oxygen,
  Crops failed,
  Cities flooded,
  Stock markets tumbled,
  Money became worthless,
  Banks collapsed,
  Armed gangs monopolised supplies.
For three years, people fought over land, storehouses, water and livestock,
  Addicts died,
  The sick were euthanized,
  The storehouses became empty as dogs ate dogs,
  The strong became the new weak.
  Retribution took its toll,
  Those who had been wealthy died valueless,
  Some architects of greed were suffocated on throats stuffed with banknotes.
After five years 95 per cent of the human species had perished,

The air stank with the smell of death,
Illness and epidemics took their toll,
The world population fell to about 1 million.
Only cooperation offered a chance of survival,
Practical skills became the new currency,
There was nothing left to trade but ability and knowledge.
Citadels of common sense started to prevail,
Politics and power had failed,
Communities began to succeed.
Earth relented a little,
Some fish appeared,
Some birds flew,
Some crops grew,
The rain became cleaner.
Wealth had been power and now there was no wealth,
The rich had died when they lost their wealth, power and respect,
Most humans died having never enjoyed wealth, power or skill,
A few survived through good health, skill and ability.
Specialisation enabled trading,
Trading demanded currency,
But currency tempted wealth and wealth tempted greed.
People resisted control,
Individual credits became the norm,
Respect could be earned but did not put food on the table,
Weapons did not make you strong any more.
The silent voices approved.

The Funeral of Democracy, Dorchester 2011

During 2010 and 2011, I became part of a protest movement against what we thought was a very unpopular and undemocratic decision made by West Dorset District Council to move their council offices to a new site. This, in our opinion, was not only hard to justify when the country was experiencing unprecedented cuts in services, but also would mean the construction of a huge building alongside a row of beautiful chestnut trees which constitute The Walks.

A protest march was organised by the Town Crier, Alistair Chisholm, who has since been elected as a councillor. A notable criminal lawyer made a speech condemning the whole episode and spoke in very strong terms about the lack of democracy.

I was moved to expressing my own disgust in the following poem which I wrote at the time the march was being planned and was read out to about 1500 people by Alistair in his inimitably powerful voice before we strode through town. This was a great honour.

Jilted lovers please take note,
The funeral date has now been wrote.

Please join the mourners of that girl
And give her life a final twirl.

We'll gather sadly come that day
And raise our placards, have our say.
We'll show our tears and fret and frown
At how it feels to be let down.

It's hard to be just second-best,
But things might change when she's put to rest.
Let's march through town down High Street West
Whose councillors have failed life's test.

But we'll make sure we throw no stones,
Instead we'll safely bear her bones
And guard our loved one wreathed in black
From those who stabbed her in the back.

We'll march to Charles Street, find the site,
Erect her stone and on it write:
'Look over there towards South Walks –
In that huge building power stalks,

'It's now the symbol of autocracy
And caused the death of our democracy.
Remember that it was your duty
To protect that goddess and her beauty.'

Percy's Blockbusters

Percy was always enthusiastic about everything he did. The confidence he displayed in every one of his ventures astonished his friends, since real achievement rarely came his way. Nevertheless, he continued throughout his life trying to do everything with an optimism which bore no relation to his actual talents.

Writing had become his latest attempt to find fame and fortune. He joined a writers' group in his home town and produced half-decent short stories at the rate of one a fortnight with his fellow enthusiasts. Like all budding authors, Percy thought his efforts were more interesting and unusual than those of his peers, but he was always encouraging and generous in his comments about the other stories when each of them read out their work. The stories were fairly short – about 600 words. If you were unkind, you might say that it was just an opportunity for some mutual adoration.

The fact that the group was led by a skilled student of English with good interpersonal skills meant that no one, including Percy, ever felt put down or treated less than magnanimously. They usually left invigorated after the two-hour sessions, feeling challenged and determined to improve and perhaps in time become a published writer, the dream of every amateur scribe.

After a year or so, Percy decided to try and get his own short stories, or at least one of them, published. He tried entering some of them for the Bridport Prize Competition and submitted manuscripts to various magazines as well as to 20 or 30 book publishers who favoured the short story genre. Their apparent inability to recognise his obvious talent disappointed him; not one editor favoured his work with an offer. Even those publishers who worked in the area of partnership publishing, where costs and profits were shared by both parties, failed to make him an offer and provide the approbation he felt he merited.

Eventually, in the absolute certainty that he could attract sufficient interest by using an unusual method, he approached a manufacturer of toilet paper and asked for a quotation to print his stories sequentially on their toilet paper. Percy convinced the managing director that the company had nothing to lose; he would be bearing the printing costs and, if nothing else, the sales of toilet rolls might even be improved. What's more, Percy discovered that the cost of printing two or three of his short stories onto each of 100,000 toilet rolls amounted to less than the cost of producing a mere 10,000 copies of a book specifically designed to attract the mass market. He and the chairman of the company reached an agreement: Percy would receive 10 per cent of the profit on any increase in sales attributed to his idea. Percy envisaged that the resultant publicity would bring him recognition and fame.

In due course, the first edition hit the toilets. Purchasers of lavatory paper usually fail to read what is printed on the wrapping paper of toilet articles so missed reading the new description informing customers that they could now read a story while they waited, so to speak! Naturally enough, the language used to convey this piece of good news to their clientele was not obvious and cloaked in a somewhat subtle way.

Before very long the press picked up on this unique product and it started to be discussed on TV chat shows and news programmes. Its originator, Percy, was interviewed live. It took only a week for some bright hack at the *News of the World* to nickname these particular products as 'Percy's Blockbusters', with obvious connotations. The actual stories which he had written were mildly amusing and some were even romantic in content. That very fact made the readers laugh at the ignominy: how, for instance, could they keep a straight face when reading a passionate love story perched on the lavatory?

Some very strange outcomes were observed after a month or so. Sales of 'Percy's Blockbusters' rocketed, followed by a major downturn in sales of laxatives. This was reported in the *Financial Times* by Boots and other leading pharmaceutical companies. These phenomena were ascribed to two suppositions.

One was that the toilet paper on which Percy's stories were printed was being consumed twice as quickly as ordinary products of that nature due to the fact that people were reading more sheets of paper at a sitting than they consumed by actually wiping their bottoms on them.

London University provided further illumination when their Sociology Department appointed a researcher to develop theories on the subject. He surmised that merely engaging oneself in reading human interest stories during one's normal daily evacuation process could reduce constipation significantly. In fact, a year later, an article in the *British Medical Journal* reported this to be true. It seemed that opening oneself (no pun intended) to the normal emotions which accompany reading subjective accounts of life and human nature was a good thing. The anal retentives who resorted to doing so thus reduced their anxiety levels to such an extent that straining was much reduced and associated problems such as haemorrhoids were also alleviated. Like most anxieties, they disappear quickly by relaxing.

Percy and the manufacturer quickly registered a Trade Mark Application for the name 'Percy's Blockbusters'. When accused by the Patent Office, they insisted that no *double entendre* was implied. In retrospect, it is difficult to believe that such a suggestion could have been made, let alone justified, even if these new short story barons had decided to state specifically on the wrapping paper that certain medicinal or psychological benefits were forthcoming if people used their product.

New sales techniques had to be invented by Percy and his partners to resist the competition from other manufacturers. For instance, they started their own publishing business, aimed strictly at short story writers. Budding writers could almost be guaranteed a place in posterity, not to mention the public's posteriors, if they were successful in being offered a contract. Customers were encouraged to collect coupons which identified various stories they had read on their toilet paper, and these could be used to obtain discounted supplies when their toilets had consumed a complete anthology of stories attributed to a particular author.

Because so many couples were getting involved in domestic arguments relating to the difficulties of simultaneously reading different stories or even the same story at different speeds, 'his and her', 'his and his' and 'her and her' twin toilet paper dispensers became the norm. Even this didn't overcome the problems associated with people competing each morning to get to the bathroom first. One difficulty in the workplace was the fact that workers were absent on toilet breaks for much longer than normal due to the way they quickly became preoccupied with the latest episodes. Some even traded them with each other like children collecting Pokémon cards.

Needless to say, hell was to pay if supplies of toilet paper were delivered out of chronological order to buyers. This resulted in frustration at gaps in stories being read or the disclosure of endings before a story had arrived at its conclusion. This could act as a constipating factor due to stress build-up, but paradoxically proved to be a bonus to employers since it brought an unexpected cost reduction: their employees started to bring their own toilet rolls to work.

Even established authors of novels began serialising their books in toilet rolls. Sewage treat-ment plants became overwhelmed with the amount of paper blocking the filtration processes. It seems that Percy's Blockbusters had shifted blockages downstream. Because toilet paper was often wasted in a mad search to find a particular chapter or serial, several rolls of pristine paper could be wasted before a user found the chapter he wanted.

Percy had become very rich before the government banned, on environmental grounds, the industry he had conceived. A Downing Street official leaked the fact that the ban was only because of the pressure from the industrialists who had suffered most by the distraction of the general public.

Although Percy was unable to claim that he had been a successful writer in the true sense of the word, he did bring joy and happiness to what for centuries had been a rather mundane part of our lives. In the process of becoming famous he also found himself a wife, but was always quick to assert that she had only become attracted to him because of his literary skills. His new-found wealth at the age of 75 and the fact that she was only 19 years old were only coincidental. In fact, they related their love affair with photographs of their marriage on a special edition of their own super-soft tissue rolls, much to the dismay of *Look* magazine.

In his heyday, after a drink or two at the annual presentation of the Percy Short Story Prize, a golden book mounted on a silver lavatory seat, he would point out to some of the equally talented people present that some stories were so badly written, he wouldn't wipe his backside on them. After all, the Percy Prize was now the only authentic seal of approval in the new dawn of popular fiction.

Oh Dear

Ernest and Mabel turned up at the doctor's after a somewhat confused journey: they had twice forgotten where they were supposed to be that morning and only arrived after first visiting the dental surgeon and the optician.

Dr Robinson was attentive to their problem and sympathetic. 'Look, I know you two are worried about memory loss, but it comes with old age and there are ways to reduce the anxiety.'

'What ways are there?' asked Ernest.

'Write everything down,' said the doctor.

'Everything?'

'Yes. It's good to get in the habit as soon as possible to avoid any confusion and possible disagreement. Always keep a notepad in your pocket or purse and make a sort of diary for everything.'

The aging couple reluctantly agreed and returned home somewhat disappointed that a medicine had not been prescribed for their condition.

After lunch, Mabel asked Ernest what he would like for pudding. 'Are there any strawberries left; the ones we bought at the market?'

'I'm sure there are.'

'I'll have some of those then.'

'All right, dear,' she said, leaving to go to the kitchen.

'Hold on.'

'What's the matter?'

'You know what the doctor said. Write it down!'

'I know my memory isn't very good, but that's ridiculous,' she retorted, and left, slamming the door behind her.

A minute later she was back. 'Anyway, what do you want on them, cream or ice cream?'

'You know I always have cream! Look, do as the doctor suggests and write it down.' He jumped up and thrust a bit of paper and his biro into her hand.

'If you think I'm going to walk round the house all day writing down silly little things like that, you've another think coming, you silly old fart.' She threw the paper and pen on the sofa and once more departed angrily.

Before he could re-engage with the daily crossword puzzle she was back again. 'You know those glace cherries we had for the Christmas cake?'

'Of course I do,' he said suspiciously.

'Shall I put a few of those on top of the cream?'

He softened. 'That's a lovely idea, dear. Very thoughtful indeed. Don't get angry with me again, but do write it down. The sooner we get in the habit of writing things down the sooner we will stop silly journeys like this morning when we get to town and don't know why we are there.'

'I'll start tomorrow. I promise,' she said, leaving serenely.

Time passed and Ernest read for the fifth time the clue which was supposed to guide him to the answer to 1 across. After about 15 minutes he became aware of the background noise coming from the kitchen.

Plates and pans were clattering, drawers were being opened and closed and Mabel was singing to herself. Eventually, she appeared at the door with a tray bearing a freshly baked apple tart and a jug of steaming hot custard.

Ernest jumped to his feet. 'What the hell is that?' he asked.

'What you asked for! I've a good mind to throw it in the bin, you ungrateful man. And one thing you can forget about right now is your Friday night cuddle.'

'I told you to write everything down but you wouldn't listen, would you. I wanted some cheddar cheese and biscuits. I might as well get it myself now.'

'Well write it down before you go.'

'BINGO!' they shouted together.

To Thine Own Self Be True

The engineering director of the Formula One racing team paused before his trophy cabinet where a tiny model car nestled ignominiously. His thoughts drifted back to 40 years ago.

It was winter and a shabbily dressed youth peered through the open door of a ramshackle garage. An old man was working on the engine of a dilapidated car.

The man paused, looked up, and after a moment's consideration said, 'You might as well come in as stand there, lad.'

The youth shuffled in, his hands deep in the pockets of his threadbare coat.

'You look cold. Can you make tea?' the man said.

'I suppose so.'

'Why not make us both a brew? All the gear is there on the table.'

The youth made the tea and the man stopped work. They sat wordlessly at an old card table and sipped from cracked cups. The man gave the youth a sandwich from a paper bag and watched him devour it hungrily, then went back to his work.

The youth rinsed the cups at the dirty sink and then moved closer to watch.

'Can I do anything?'

'You can help if you want.'

The man explained what he was doing and the youth did as he was asked. As they proceeded, he was able to help his mentor more and more. By mid-afternoon they managed to start the car engine. The man decided another cup of tea was in order and they once more sat at the table. More sandwiches were shared.

The man said, 'Tell me what your problems are.'

The youth kept his eyes down.

'I don't know what to do with my life. I'm always in trouble. I hate school. I should be there now.'

'What do your mother and father say about it?'

'Dad's in gaol and my mum's a drug addict. We survive on handouts from the SS.'

'That can't be very nice.'

'No. The trouble is, I don't know where to turn.'

There was a pause.

'I think you've made a start already.'

'How's that?'

'You've found something that interests you. One interest can lead to another as you grow older, and before you know it you will have a career. This old car interests you. You could try to get some proper training and eventually find work doing something you like.'

'It can't be that easy.'

'Take one step at a time. Decide what makes you feel good in life; it's usually better than feeling important. Search for what you need and be true to yourself without necessarily running with the crowd. Perhaps consider asking your headmaster for some training in mechanical engineering. Most importantly, listen to what people including me tell you, and then think hard and make up your own mind. Anyway, it's time I went.'

'Will you be here tomorrow?'

'I'm not sure where I'll be, but I'm usually about somewhere or other. You'll find me if you need to.'

'Oh,' said the youth, rather puzzled. 'Well, goodbye then, and thanks for the tea and sandwiches.'

'You're welcome.'

The youth sauntered out but he'd been gone only a few minutes before he hurried back in through the open door. He was forming the words, 'How can I contact you, then?' before he realised that he was addressing an empty shed. A pile of rusting scrap metal marked the spot where the car had been. The man was nowhere to be seen.

He stood in perplexed thought until his fingers encountered a foreign object in his coat pocket. He smiled when he found it was a tiny replica of the car he had helped to start. He walked through the darkening streets with a new sense of purpose.

The Cost of Everything and the Value of Nothing

The Master of Plight (sometimes called the Human Condition) called a summit meeting.

'I'm not happy the way things are going,' he stated ominously. 'I'm getting some very bad reports from Earth and I need a full account of your activities. Every-thing, you can go first. You appear to be all things to mankind,' he added sarcastically.

'Well, Master, I've tried to satisfy everyone on this planet since our last meeting in 1850 and made the world a better place to live in. Look at the joy people take in the things I've brought here. There's Viagra for the young and toys for the old, for instance!'

The Master snorted derisively. Unfazed, Every-thing continued, 'There are new developments in technology, computer games where humans can battle it out in virtual reality. Cars go faster, food is tastier, sex is sexier, travel is easier, watches tell the time to a millisecond, there's TV and films to see every minute of the day, clothes of every colour, holidays in exotic places, expense accounts...'

'Enough!' The Master interrupted. 'Your turn, Cost. I hope your act has more general appeal.'

'Master, I must say that without Every-thing's efforts, my life would be very dull. However, I have been able to exact a high price for his gifts. His recipients have paid up generously in terms of envy, greed, conspicuous ownership, loss of silence and pride. Also they have developed an overwhelming capacity to judge themselves only in terms of whom they know, what they possess and how much they can drink, which are further indications of my success. For everything that Every-thing has supplied, I have responded appropriately with my own scale of charges. Paradoxically, every recipient of his seductive merchandise has coughed up uncomplainingly with suffering and hardship.'

'Enough self-praise, Cost! You'll be whipping yourself next to make up for it.'

'But Master, I haven't yet mentioned some of my other charges: venereal disease, depression and fifty-mile-long traffic jams.'

'Sit down, Cost! You're next, No-thing. Can you hear me? Give her a prod, someone.'

No-thing came to and started to sing.

'Got no diamonds, got no pearl,

'Still I think I'm a lucky girl

'I've got the sun in the morning and the moon at night.

'Sunshine gives me a lovely day

'Moonlight gives me the Milky Way.'

'*Stop that noise*, No-thing! Have you gone mad?'

She spoke sweetly. 'Sorry, Master but if Every-thing didn't exist, there would be no need for that other arch-villain, Cost! I expect they think that because I am No-thing that I don't count in the general scheme of things. But...', becoming lyrical, 'I am left over after they cause meltdown. I am the calmness which

48

follows the storm, the tranquillity which follows chaos, the simplicity which follows complexity, the truth that follows lies ...', breaking into song again, 'the sun in the morning and the stars at night. Moonlight...'

'*Shut up* No-thing. Go back to your silent meditation or we'll soon be in Cuckooland with your converts. Value, for my own sanity, please try and make some sense.'

'Thank you, Master,' he began, speaking pompously, tossing his dreadlocks over his shoulders and speaking in a North American twang. 'Unlike the others, I try to be everywhere and make small inroads instead of going for outright domination. I bring balance and choice. It's to do with teaching people to use their hearts instead of their heads, their feelings instead of their thoughts and their imaginations instead of the dubious certainties offered by the others. We all know what happens without my mediation – there is a spirituelle and materielle desert out there and all we really need is lurv, man.'

'Don't get carried away, Value, you don't seem to have made much difference where you come from,' said the Master. 'However, things could be worse. I remember what happened to Mars when we left it to No-one, Use-less and Value-less. You know what I want from all of you: cooperation, equilibrium and sustainability. Get on with it everybody! I'll see you in 2500.'

On Being Assertive

George breathed a sigh of relief and settled himself behind the wheel of his car. He turned on his satellite navigation system and entered his home address. 'Take over Charles,' he said. 'Get me out of this rat race.'

He surrendered to the luxury of not having to look at a map or even think about the route and left it entirely to Charles. He had nicknamed the satnav Charles when he first bought the car, since the verbal instructions were male and reassuring. They seemed to contrast with the female option: 'she' was very patronising and tended to sarcasm when saying, for instance, 'If possible, make a U-turn.'

Over the years, Charles had become company on dark nights and a blessing on days when he was gutted with tiredness and feeling needy. Road junctions came and went and George followed Charles's instructions faithfully.

'At the roundabout, take the third exit.'
'In half a mile turn right.'
'In one mile, turn right to join the motorway.'
And so on …

George let his thoughts turn to his life and his many failures due to his lack of assertiveness. He talked out loud. 'I'm a weasel and always scared to stand up to people. I never argue with anyone; that would mean making a decision. Actually being rude enough to say to someone they were in the wrong would scare the life out of me.'

'Go on!' boomed out of the loudspeakers.

George jumped several inches.

He pressed a button on the steering wheel for a repeat of Charles's last instruction.

'In one mile, turn right to join the motorway.'

'I must be going mad, Charles. I thought you said something quite different. Anyway what difference would it make if you did? What a hopeless fool I am – married twice, a complete jerk, a low-grade salesman with a low-grade product. I wish I could be different: assertive, commanding, successful.'

'Go on,' boomed Charles.

'What?'

'I said go on.'

'You never say that to me.'

'If possible, make a U-turn.'

'No way! I'm doing 80 miles per hour on the M3!'

'Now you're talking!'

'I think you've got hold of a computer virus. Either that or I'm completely mad.'

'You're not mad and I haven't got the flu.'

George drove silently for some minutes thinking that he now had delusional behaviour to add to his many faults. He was tempted to switch Charles off .

'I can help you make a U-turn, George,' startled him again.

'You really are talking to me, aren't you?'

'Leave the motorway at the next exit'

George obeyed.

'Leave me switched on. Always talk to me. When I approve, you will hear "At the next junction, go straight on." If I don't, you will hear, "If possible make a U-turn." Ask me questions. I will answer "Turn right" if I agree with you, or "Turn left" if I don't.'

Over the next months, a slow change took place in George's demeanour. He became involved and more active at work. He took time with his appearance. He listened more carefully to others and spoke with a sense of purpose. More importantly, he became fun to be with and laughed a lot. He got a new girlfriend.

On his promotion to regional sales manager, he was provided with a brand new BMW. He spoke quietly to Charles before leaving his old vehicle at a car sales depot.

'Thanks, Charles, you were a great friend.'

'Turn right,' said Charles.

George sadly turned off the ignition and the satnav screen faded. As he opened the door, he heard Charles say, 'At the next junction, go straight on,' but already he was putting the episode down to his imagination.

Well, wouldn't you?

Sugar

Sugar's sweet I've heard it said, like daytime sex
    in another's bed,
But if skies outside are full of rain and
    consciences are under strain,
Ignoring storms might be in vain.

Is sugar sour or sweet, I ask?
But do we want to take to task what we've been
    taught
and see the proof our faces are just masks?
We can always use the leader's eyes and put our
    trust in paradise,
But that's just hiding truth in lies.

We germinate the seeds young minds acquire;
To raise a hand could risk hell fire for those
    whose teachers were unkind.
'Smith, are you stupid or just blind?
Just follow the rules and don't enquire, or face
    expulsion from life's choir.'

Are we erect or on all fours?
Pursuing lives on many floors
of houses full of hidden doors?
As frightened couples closely curled we leave
    our questions tightly furled,
Avoiding hits from gauntlets hurled.

Last night I tried philosophy to fill a space,
A target for my ego's chase.
The venture ended miserably when work gave
    way to a soft settee
With a drink to suit – unsweetened tea.
I listened to McCartney's plea,
'Let it be, let it be, let it be'.

It's quite a gift, said a famous scribe,
To see ourselves as others see us.
There was no gibe,
So what's the fuss?
But will I get into a lather if I see myself as my
    son's father?
Oh, there's my bus.
Who gives a cuss?

First Days

The train spewed an odd mixture of male humanity onto a misty, cold, Oswestry station. Most faces bore signs of apprehension but no time was available for introspection since we were quickly loaded into trucks taking us to our camp for the next two months.

There was time for everyone to be kitted out before supper, which was surprisingly good. The rigours of bullshit soon became a reality as we learned to polish boots like mirrors and Blanco our webbing. God knows why it was ever called Blanco since it more closely resembles the colour of the Ganges after a monsoon with a generous introduction of human waste.

There were other enigmas that we became familiar with during our training. If we were considered to be lazy, inefficient or just plain useless we were given a 'bending', either individually or collectively. This had nothing to do with one's back as the term might suggest, but more with making its recipients bend to the will of their instructors. Offenders were made to perform exercises to the point of exhaustion: 50 press-ups was a common sentence. The NCOs replaced God's position of power in our lives. Ironically, given the amount of spontaneous obeisance the process generated, it probably proved more efficient than school assembly prayers.

Eventually, we became a well-knit and fit group of young men, albeit sex-starved, short of cigarettes and mostly feeling knackered. One weekend I allowed boredom to overtake my sense of realism and made the mistake of sparring with another recruit who boxed for Northern Universities. My next error was to seize an opportunity to clock him good and proper with a right cross. That resulted in a wilting series of blows to my chin and an early submission on my part. Since from that point on I ceased showing any bravery, I was surprised that the incident evoked some respect for me from the PE instructors. Perhaps it was sympathy!

One morning, I awoke feeling like death with all the symptoms of flu: headache, aching bones, high temperature. With what I have now come to accept is a facet of my personality which can have widely varying effects on those around me, I told my barrack-room friends that I had decided to stay in bed for the day. I realised afterwards that what I perceived on their faces was not empathy but fear for my safety. My defying the only force in our lives at that time was clearly worrying them.

For the next hour, despite my discomfort, I snuggled down in blissful silence until my demeanour was roughly disturbed by an NCO who materialised screaming in rage and disbelief. I waited patiently for his brainstorm to subside before asking him to send for the doctor. This request initiated such a display of incandescence and foul language on his part that I decided to accept his explanation that the only reason a medical officer would visit the barrack-room was to certify my death. I got dressed slowly despite the man's impatience. I followed him outside, where to my surprise he ordered me to run at the double to the surgery.

This was the last straw. As calmly as possible, I told him no way was I going to run anywhere, so he could please himself. I stoically walked the rest of the way, leaving him fuming. The MO took my temperature before giving me a large tablet to swallow – known, I discovered later, as a Number 9 Pill. I was told I was on light duties for the rest of the day, so I returned to my billet and went back to bed. Whatever was in a No 9 pill certainly did the trick, since my recovery was rapid.

My only claim to fame during an otherwise ignominious two months was being in charge of the only field gun to hit dead centre a rock 2 miles away with a 25 pound shell.

Some other episodes come to mind. We were allowed into town for one night as a reward for passing out. I did just that, literally, through an excess of alcohol. I received a photo from my girlfriend to remind me how stunning she was, which I still have. She was absolutely beautiful in those days. I met her recently and was somewhat disappointed to find that life had not been kind either to her or her looks. This was a lesson to me that in future, I shouldn't leave my valuable possessions lying about where they could be stolen.

BINGO

Beauty is mercurial, difficult to identify, label or describe; perhaps enhanced by desire but certainly corrupted by fear. Does it depend on emotion for survival? A stormy sea is easily enjoyed from the comfort of a warm sitting room with a good meal and half a bottle of wine in your stomach. Shipwrecked starving mariners might not share that view. Are we guided by our instincts to those we find to be beautiful on grounds which are peculiar to us? Others may fall in love with people we perceive to be cosmetically plain individuals. Are we like climbers needing a sense of danger and insecurity to make risky mountains a beautiful challenge?

Integrity. Is it our trustworthiness or sense of honesty which earns this label? Is the word related to 'integer' which is the name given to any whole number. Does integrity imply wholeness as a person? Does safety with someone and complete trust give us an impression of integrity. Is it a case of how we feel about someone or what we know of their activities? Can we feel safe in one area but not in another? Or, is it something more basic and elusive, not dependant necessarily on one's actions or the feelings which they inspire but rather the sense that the individual with integrity is open to the world and aware of his shortcomings.

Normality. Does such a thing exist? Abnormality disturbs, frightens or threatens many. Normality can be depressing for others who yearn for a change in their existence if only to bring an end to their boredom. Can we recognise boredom or uncertainty without the assistance of our innate feelings which give us a sense of either security or fear and vary with our environment? How can we feel so secure and strong that we can view each experience as being something wondrous and new giving our full intelligence and attention to its detail? Is it possible to do this or are we governed forever to make the same decisions about situations as we always have done. But given absolute freedom to have ourselves re-programmed, would we have the courage to do so? This is a crucial question since by doing so we would be committing ourselves to see the world differently and not necessarily as it is.

Gifts. What is a gift, something for nothing? Is a gift worth having if it is something which the giver could easily afford or not miss? Is a gift an opportunity to display righteousness since the giver's friends, acquaintances or relatives will hear about it? Should all one's gifts be anonymously given so we know we are doing it for the right reasons? Of course, it would be difficult to anonymously give your wife, friend, family members or lover a gift especially since the whole reason for the gift would be to make them feel good. But, giving also makes the giver feel good according to St Francis. Is there merit in giving gifts to people we dislike? It may be even more appropriate if we are looking for self-development. Is it more or less appropriate to do this openly or anonymously? Why do we engage in the process of gifting at all? At the end of the day, wouldn't we rather that someone held us in their arms and said 'I love you', 'I love being with you', 'What can I do for you which will really make you happy?' or 'You really do annoy me and I wish there was some way we could get on better', than indulge their own ideas of what is going to be good for us?

Over. Does over mean over? Yes!

Beauty, Integrity, Normality, Gifts and Over. BINGO! Thank goodness for that!

Are We an Epilogue or a Preface?

From cradle to grave, our personalities mutate in response to our experience. Most of us are defined by our pasts and to varying degrees moulded at birth. One might fondly imagine that we all have the free will to become whatever we wish in a world full of opportunity. However, our random genetic blueprints and the people we descend from remain the main determinants of our future. Our close families play a huge part in our development, for better or worse. Their wealth, poverty, education or ignorance can determine our character, temperament and future existence. It's difficult to avoid the statistical evidence which shows that 70 per cent of our prison population come from broken homes or worse. Parental position and privilege provide, not unexpectedly, many opportunities to the more fortunate.

Despite these rather obvious reasons why we could easily resign ourselves to fate, many of us look to changing our identities in some way rather than feeling trapped in what sociologists would construe as our societal 'roles'. I wonder if the real reason behind the growth in virtual reality games is down to this need to reinvent ourselves as avatars of our choosing without disturbing our old and seemingly safer habits in the real world.

As competent adults, we can sometimes overlook the enormous effect we have on each other's development and self-realisation. We all know the limitations or aspirations our backgrounds arrange for us, but it is how we react to and cooperate with one another which can determine whether we will treat our lives as merely epilogues to a continuing mundane existence, or as prefaces which prepare the ground for us to launch ourselves, whatever our ages and backgrounds, into unimaginably exciting and mysterious futures.

Change is difficult for most of us because we fear it. If we become altered, our close friends and family become upset without knowing why. But any changes we make will change their lives too, however slightly, and make them in turn feel threatened. We seek reassurance from time to time by looking up old cronies to look at life in similar ways.

Our fears may affect our social mobility: we can feel out of place in the presence of powerful people or subject to contamination if we get too close to the poor and needy. We are all products of each other but in the main reflect our self-images rather than face the uncertainty of the unknown by risking change. We can stumble through life as though we have no options. I came to the conclusion some time ago that for someone to achieve really big changes in his life and to seek new horizons of ambition and hope, he would need to change his environment completely. What makes this easier to understand is how relaxed and uninhibited we can become with total strangers. They accept whatever we are, and we do the same for them. The trick then is not to rewrite our old identities.

Christmas is the time of the year when family reunions can reconfirm old identities, and for many can become a tribulation instead of perhaps an occasion for rejoicing in the changes we have sought and made in our lives. We are always in danger of projecting our own insecurities and fears onto our fellow souls. This is an irony given that the birth of Jesus is meant to represent forgiveness for the past and hope for a new life.

Perhaps the best way of accomplishing this will be to try to accept people as they are, and any changes they make as a challenge to our own insecurities. By helping one another through our fears we will all be liberated. Can we adopt this as a new project?

I once had the strange thought that since life is such a lottery, each of us could have been anyone. My often suspect reasoning suggests that therefore we are everyone.

Car Park Blues

Theo eased his well-cared-for but ancient Jaguar into a vacant space. He had awakened that morning with a sense of disquiet; a touch of 'the blues' you might say. He switched off the engine and sat there looking at the hundreds of empty vehicles around him.

'Cars are like epitaphs,' he thought to himself. 'They tell you something about their owners. I suppose everyone wants his identity to be recognised. We like to let others know who we are. You can tell a lot about people from the cars they drive. Anyone looking at my car would know I am lonely and middle-aged. Of course, they wouldn't know that with the right sort of woman beside me, I could be less like Victor Meldrew!'

He viewed a new arrival as its owner searched for a vacant spot. 'No problem with that car, for instance. They're probably short of cash and both unemployed. Maybe two kids, stressed out and signs of strain in their marriage.

'Now that one's owners are quite different. They're clearly well-heeled. Could be from Sherb'n', he said out loud with an affected upper-class accent. 'They wouldn't think of shopping in Tesco and I'd put money on the fact he's wearing a suit and she buys £30 worth of ingredients to make a fish pie. And tells their guests how much they spent on it, too.' He shook his head in disgust and turned his attention to a car parked nearby.

'That's an easy one. Clearly it belongs to some smart-arse from London. Probably he's down for the weekend having made another half-million in bonuses in the City. He'll no doubt have his new squeeze with him wearing her latest outfit and they can't wait to get to their hotel. Lucky sods!'

When people returned to their cars, Theo wasn't surprised to find that that most of his predictions appeared correct. He became so immersed in these speculations that he was startled when someone tapped loudly on his nearside window. He lowered the glass.

'Can you possibly help me? I've stupidly locked my keys and purse in the boot.'

Theo immediately got out and went round to talk to her. 'I'll try,' he said as he took in her appearance, thinking as he did so that no way had he associated any of the cars with this very attractive woman. 'Which is your car?'

'It's the old Triumph over there.'

Since he had gained so much experience restoring various vintage motor cars, with the help of his own toolbox he was able to open her boot after ten minutes or so, pleased to see the relief flooding her face. They swapped stories for a few moments about previous cars they had owned. He asked what had brought her to Dorset and she told him she had come to look at houses for sale since she had divorced recently and was hoping to make a new start.

Over coffee, they found they shared some interests

and hobbies. By lunchtime, they couldn't stop smiling.

Later, dining together, she made a confession.

'I've been very dishonest, Theo.'

'How's that, Janet?'

'Well, I watched you in the car park for quite a while and decided you looked a nice man and were possibly a bit lonely like me. So, I faked my problem with the car keys. I had a spare one in my pocket.'

Theo laughed. 'I've a confession too. I could quite easily have just pulled the back seat forward and retrieved your keys but I wanted to seem more of a Galahad and also get to know you better.'

Six months later found them living together in Sherborne and occasionally eating fish pies containing expensive ingredients. They say love changes everything!

Grains

Building castles, sunny days, scratchy eyes and
 itchy toes.
In fading sun and warmly soothed, I kiss and
 stroke my autumn rose,
We walk back home, hand clasped in hand.
Oh how I loved those grains of sand.

Crowds are heaving, smells enticing, natives
 talking, bodies sweating,
Memsahibs preening, mad dogs leering,
 rickshaws speeding, three-card betting –
Bangkok enthrals me. Brown girls are nice, why
 think of vice?
I bump into a long-lost friend. Against the odds
 in grains of rice.

Makes you thirsty, dries out white, you need a bit
 to stay alive.
It's nice on chips, you lick your lips. But eat too
 much and you won't thrive.
Oceans, lotions, potions, motions, beaches,
 leeches. I'll call a halt.
Why make an essay like a dolt about a million
 grains of salt?

I know you're right and I am too. We're men of
    wisdom, me and you,
We've got the nous and know the answers,
    solving riddles on the loo.
I wonder sometimes what we'd do if we
    answered questions in a booth
And countless women queued to see us as we
    dished out grains of truth.
Pinch ourselves most likely!

All I Remember After That Was ...

Water lapped against the steel hull of the narrowboat and warm summer rain beat against its roof. Beer and sandwiches at the riverside pub had completed my idea of heaven and I settled down on my bed for a siesta now that my wife, daughter and our friends had departed to look round a village.

I awoke to my wife screaming hysterically, 'What the hell are you doing sleeping? Get up!'

'I'm entitled to sleep if I want. Why don't you all clear off to the village as you promised and let me get some rest!'

At that point the forward door of our cabin burst open and my friend Roger collapsed onto the floor, clutching his head. He was wearing waterproofs and a sou'wester. They were bright yellow – apart from the blood that was.

Since my wife was clearly having a nervous breakdown and Roger was understandably not feeling very talkative, I wrapped a towel round his head and ignoring my wife's continuing screams, rather irritably went aft to see if his wife Jennifer and our daughter Sarah were also part of this madhouse. I found them fast asleep in the stern. For some unaccountable reason, the boat was in midstream and motoring rudderless towards a large weir.

I realised this was just another normal day in our week's boating holiday. We had already survived a complete electrical failure, Roger breaking the rudder against some lock gates, sucking a large waterlogged carpet into the prop shaft and me falling overboard twice one night in pitch darkness. Why worry? I put the engine into reverse and applied full power to avoid a watery grave. Ten minutes later, we were tied up safely against the bank of the River Avon.

I returned to Roger, relieved him of his rain gear and settled him comfortably with a couple of para-cetamols before waking the two sleeping beauties. It was time to attempt a normal conversation with Kath, who was still in a state of shock. Of course, like all bad dreams this one had an explanation based on reality. What had happened was this ...

We had stopped at a boatyard that morning for urgent repairs. The engineer arrived and started work so we all went to a local pub for lunch. I decided it was too rainy to go walking and returned to the boat for a snooze. The other four carried on exploring the local village.

Roger and his wife brought our daughter back first and relaxed in the saloon. Amazingly, despite Roger's habit of snoring, they must have all dropped off, since they were fast asleep when Kath returned. The engineer then started the engine, engaged the propeller and jumped ashore. His final words as he cast us off were 'You'll be OK now.' Little did he realise!

Kath didn't see the significance of his actions until she realised she was surrounded by comatose people and motoring downstream. Not being technical, her first action was to wake up Roger and tell him the good news. Despite Kath's impatience, he insisted on first donning full marine weather gear including a sou'wester. It was raining cats and dogs. However, he then rushed forward through my cabin and climbed the stairs to the foredeck at full speed. Since sightseeing cannot have been on his mind, I could only suppose he must have forgotten that the engine was in the stern.

Clearly, his view was now obstructed by his headgear since his head struck the hatch, which was closed to keep out the rain. Bleeding profusely from a head wound, he fell back down into the stairwell. Game to the end, he burst into my cabin before collapsing at the foot of my bed.

This is where I came in!

A Visit to a Special Place

It's 1943. I'm ten years old. Days of heavy rain had filled the well in the garden of a pebble-dashed bungalow in Laindon, Essex. Now the sun is shining and when I pull up a bucket of water, sunlight turns the splashes to liquid silver. I sit on the outside commode, hidden behind an ill-fitting door. Squares of newspaper hang on a hook. The smell of human waste blends with summer scents and insects hum outside. The flies are impatient for me to leave.

My Gran makes breakfast – fried herrings. Small bones are ignored and chased down with home-made bread and butter. Sometimes we have eggs from hens she has reared on her own potatoes. I boil them for her on a paraffin stove as an excuse to secretly gorge on their waxy, iron taste and wish I was a chicken.

A V1 'flying bomb' drones overhead. If the engine stops we will dive under the table, but it continues like an angry wasp to end some lives elsewhere. After Gran has departed to the shops pushing an old pram, I walk in flower-strewn woods but can still hear the crump of explosions coming from London. By chance, I meet a girl in there, lonely like me. She's leggy with long hair. After we have found some common ground, we kiss timidly and hold hands, but my mother appears. Her silent disapproval abruptly ends my chances of unimaginable intimacy. I think, 'Never mind, I can flatten a penny on the railway line after dinner.' Years later we meet again. She has become vivacious and lost her innocence and I have lost my appeal.

Before Grandad leaves for his nightly visit to listen to Churchill on his friend's wireless, he invites me to sleep in his Anderson shelter. I wake the next day covered with huge spiders and find myself standing on the front lawn shaking with fright. He says, 'They won't hurt you', holding one which wriggles through his fingers. I decide it's safer to risk Hitler's bombs in future.

One afternoon, Gran shows me life-like drawings of Zulu warriors and Red Indians. I am dumb-founded when she says, 'I can't draw to save my life. I just sit down with a pencil and close my eyes.' That night, as usual, she gives me a goodnight kiss and slips a bit of her home-made toffee into my mouth. The grandfather clock keeps me company as a mysterious light moves around the ceiling – interesting and strange but not worrying.

Our holiday over, I tag behind my sad mother through the shattered streets and lives of the East End. At 40 she is already beaten by life. The Cheltenham Flyer carries us from Paddington to the beauty of Gloucestershire but I know my final destination will make the last fortnight seem like heaven.

Ten years later, I see my Gran again. Her peace envelops me. My Grandad is dead so she no longer needs to be dutiful. She makes our dinner and listens to my news. Afterwards, she reads with difficulty through her cataracts and I watch the fire. The tick of the clock and the soft hiss of the gas lamp fill the room. An ember tumbles from the grate.

She tells me how she was born in 1869 in a village inn where horses clattered and steamed as stage coaches arrived in the courtyard. Sheep stealers were hanged from a crossroads gibbet and headless riders galloped through the night on soundless hooves.

As darkness falls, I make my way back to my regiment and the wintry Thames of Gravesend. I rue how quickly my visit is over. Gran's refuge from the world was compulsorily purchased a year later to make way for the brave new world of Basildon and the luxury of a council flat with a flush toilet. She lived for only a few more weeks.

It's 2036 and President Yaws Looks Back

From the archives

The private secretary entered the Prime Minister's office.

'Good morning, sir. Was your trip successful?'

'It all went very well, James, I must say. So well in fact that I think some champagne should be put on ice for lunchtime.'

'I'll arrange that, sir.'

'Make sure that the Press Officer spins a good story and doesn't forget to mention my leading role. Yes, we've saved some jobs in the defence industry as well as keeping our old friends happy.'

'I notice that the papers seemed to think that some palms were greased to get those orders.'

'You know the score, James. We've all got our jobs to do. Mine is the art of compromise.'

'I understand that compromise is a necessary adjunct in all negotiations, sir, but when one is dealing with an undemocratic regime, I think the rules are a little different. Only the other day, I recalled when the Americans were trying to justify the arms deals they had made with Bin Laden. There was also the matter of the gassing of thousands of people in Iraq by Saddam Hussein.'

'What's got into you today? You sound like the Archbishop of Canterbury. I'd like to see how he would cope with this job. The Synod can't even deal with the issue of homosexuality, never mind the real problems in this world.'

'I'm just commenting, sir.'

There was an awkward silence for a few moments before James cleared his throat.

'There is something else I think you might like to consider, sir.'

'Yes?' the Prime Minister responded, a little tetchily.

'The mortality rate of our soldiers in Afghanistan seems to be escalating and there are suggestions that some of their deaths are being caused by British-made weaponry.'

'How am I supposed to keep track of every bullet, James? Our streets are full of youths armed with guns made in Russia, for God's sake. I've got daily pressure to reduce unemployment, defence industries on my back asking for help to secure orders, the military after more cash and personnel. I told you, it's all a big juggle and some principles go down the drain. Now let's change the bloody subject and deal with the mail!'

'I'm disappointed, sir. You're clearly more interested in ballistics than statistics. I'll enlighten you a little. My son Robert, for instance.'

'How's he getting on? Went to Sandhurst, didn't he?'

'Yes.' A pause. 'He was killed 15 months ago in Afghanistan.'

'Oh my God. Why didn't you mention it? It must have been terrible. How have you coped?'

'Badly and in private, is the short answer. I'd hoped to be able to be proud of his sacrifice but all I can think of now is how his life was wasted. Today, you have confirmed my belief that in reality he was just a toy in this terrible playground which you and the world's leaders have constructed to act out your little games.'

'But, James ...'

'Let me continue. I've learned not only to grieve but also to ask myself if I haven't connived in his death and that of many other fine young men and women by my inaction. I see him now as just an innocent little boy who was proud to serve his country and its politicians in whom he placed his faith. My own lifelong service as a civil servant must have reinforced those views. He was misled.'

James took a piece of twisted metal from his pocket and placed it on the side table.

'This is what killed him. I used my influence – in fact, I used my position and your name – to obtain it after his body was sent back home. It was embedded in his brain. You know, when I waited at Wootton Bassett for the Hercules to land with its cargo of coffins, I was in mind that they were just commodities like boxes of apples. How I wish they were. Coxes Orange Pippins would have been much nicer,' he said wistfully.

'Anyway, that's by the way. It took me some time, but eventually I was able to identify the source of the shrapnel which killed my son. It came from the casing of an explosive device made in Birmingham! I expect you can now understand why our conversation is taking this direction.'

'But that wasn't my fault any more than that of the factory workers who made the bloody thing. Give me a break, James.'

'I agree entirely. We are all at fault. You, me, factory workers turning out peacetime weapons, weak politicians, millionaire arms dealers, weak-kneed religious leaders, the press barons and the donkeys who led our lions in the First World War. We all conspire in a very dirty business and as far as I am concerned this whole stinking political edifice is rotten through and through.'

James produced a gun and swiftly screwed a silencer onto its short barrel. The PM stood up white-faced and made as if to try and ring for help. He changed his mind and attempted to reason.

'Look, James, let's talk the whole thing through. He pointed outside. The sun's out. Let's go for a walk in the garden. I'm sure we can find a way forward here for both of us.'

'I'm afraid it's too late for that now, Prime Minister. I have no future now, no ambition or peace of mind. You will be part of the statement I am going to make.'

'Yes, what a good idea. Let's both decry the arms situation in a joint message highlighting your loss. Draft it for me. I'll do anything to prevent this sort of thing happening again.'

'You didn't listen to me properly. It's too late for false shows of righteousness now, by either of us. There is an ironic twist to the situation, though. Do you know I couldn't get hold of a British-made gun here in England? I knew your sense of patriotism would prefer it so I had to fly to Iraq where they're readily available. It will be something to dwell on during our trip to Hell.'

There was loud pop and a cloud of smoke and the bullet hit the PM in the chest. He sat back down with that same mixture of arrogance, surprise, disbelief and boyish charm which had proved so useful to him at Prime Minister's Question Time. Then his head lolled forward and his life was over.

James swiftly removed a small package which was taped to the inside of his coat and connected by wire to a tiny camera and microphone concealed in his top pocket among the usual pens and pencils. It took only a moment more to retrieve a memory stick from the recorder. He took this to the computer terminal and within a minute or two had uploaded to the internet the entire digital video recording of their discussion. The first recipient was YouTube.

When he was absolutely certain that these operations had been performed successfully, he hid all of the devices in the cistern of the lavatory in the Prime Minister's private bathroom. He then returned to his seat in front of the blood-stained corpse. He put the gun into his mouth and pulled the trigger once more. Blood, brain matter and skull fragments sprayed the ceiling. Gradually his blood pooled on the floor to join that of the Prime Minister as it flowed out from under his desk.

When their bodies were discovered, panic enveloped Downing Street. Conferences were quickly arranged to try to cover up the obvious implications. The police made their report and the bodies were taken to the Middlesex hospital for autopsies. At midday a news bulletin informed a shocked world of the tragedy, and that evening the Deputy Prime Minister sombrely appeared on TV. He explained to the nation that James had been depressed and of unsound mind due to the death of his only son and had murdered the PM before committing suicide. It was extremely upsetting but the government was now more determined than ever to stop the illegal distribution of guns which had resulted in this double tragedy.

However, the videoed details of what had happened were already in the public domain and were being watched simultaneously by millions on their laptops, PCs and mobile phones. The following weeks were chaotic. There were other suicides and large-scale resignations from workers in the defence and armaments industries. The government resigned from office and there were uprisings on an unprecedented scale around the world. The corporate offices of listed companies in the armaments sector were ransacked and vandalised. Parents of soldiers killed on active service in the Middle East trouble spots organised marches against the mendacity of politicians of all denominations. The public anger over the MPs' expense scandal resurfaced and there was an enormous backlash against the banking system and the fat-cat culture which had dominated public opinion until that point.

YouTube posthumously awarded James with its highest accolade, suggesting that it was the politics of Britain and most other countries whose sanity should really be questioned and not that of the film's maker, the humbled and saddened parent of a brave, betrayed soldier. They argued that James's personal sacrifice was comparable with that of the unarmed rebels who gave their lives in Libya, Syria and Bahrain in their fight for democracy.

President's Note
This nonsense all took place 25 years ago. I became the leader of the incoming government formed by the Party for Democratic Freedom which won a landslide victory at the subsequent General Election. The then current sense of anarchy gave the public all the encouragement they needed to ditch the royals and elect me President. With all the controls I now have in place, there's no bloody way a naive and sentimental idiot like that Private Secretary will ever pull a fast one on me! Here's to freedom – my kind that is!

U.P. Yaws

Confusion

This message was found in a bottle in 2110 and sent to the National Artefact Repository.

This morning, February 24th, 2078, I kept my MOT appointment. I am now back at home and feeling much better.

Once, people were required to have their vehicles tested annually for mechanical fitness. Now, the acronym MOT is used for the Mental Optimization Test designed to obtain an altogether different form of fitness. We don't talk about mental problems these days as if we have terrible diseases; we are merely *confused.*

It was in 2010 that a researcher submitted a thesis to the British Psychological Association explaining why so many people led unfulfilled lives whilst others were quite happy and self-realised. The psychology professionals were shocked by his simplistic approach. They had become used to blinding themselves and us with complex reasons to explain our mental shortcomings; they were reluctant to concede that even their own phobias, anxieties and depressions lessened as a result of using his methods. Of course, they later institutionalised the whole process to preserve their own status!

This man's theory was that each of us is born with congenital defects which influence the ways in which we view the world. Our upbringing can exacerbate these but usually introduces a whole range of other problems. He suggested that these ailments are akin to defective eyesight; one might say we are all equipped from birth with mental spectacles whose prescriptions are unique to every one of us. If we are lucky, the lenses remain supple and variable, constantly able to change in response to our experiences. As we grow older, one person's lenses might remain rigidly fixed in their distortion of reality while another's might distort it according to the circumstances of its owner. No one sees the world as it really is, since one's sense of reality is always distorted to a greater or lesser extent.

The researcher concluded that a group of people could, if they wished, combine their individual senses of reality and derive an average reality which would be much more accurate. To do this, they would need to determine a consensus view in a wide variety of situations.

So, he compiled a huge database detailing the subjective and objective reactions of thousands of people to countless scenarios which he had recorded as video clips and images. This made it possible for a confused person to compare his reactions to various theoretical situations with the group norm and to determine the degree of distortion affecting his own life.

This morning, my MOT report revealed that metaphorically speaking, I am still picturing certain aspects of my life as I did as a child when my lenses were newly fashioned. With the help of the database, I was able for the first time to see many situations as if I had perfect eyesight. Already, new light is entering those areas of my life which have given me most difficulty. I can now see many other ways to view the world and can start to break old habits. Hypothetically, I will be able to revisit situations wearing different spectacles. The excitement is almost too great to bear.

You might think that all we need to do is to have more friends and acquaintances to keep hold of reality. This is not necessarily so, since a recent survey showed that 95 per cent of the population now live almost permanently wired into their computers in virtual realities. This ancient MOT facility may soon close for upgrading to the latest version, which will frighteningly rewrite the memories of referred *confusees* without their consent. A few of us have determined that when that happens we will regularly get together and try to guide one another through the darkness rather than risk completely losing who we are.

Multitasking

Everyone multitasks! It's part of our education and cognitive development. But do we know what we mean when we talk of the subject?

When I started to learn to fly, it was as much as I could do to keep the aeroplane flying in a level position, never mind altering its speed or trying anything difficult like changing its direction. As my competence improved in doing simple things, I added more and more complex procedures. However, these only became possible because my brain had learned how to subdivide jobs into routines.

In the early days I can remember my instructor telling me that the Air Traffic Controller had been talking to us on and off for some time. I was embarrassed to realise that he had been communicating with him on my behalf since I had started my course. I was told to learn to listen to what was being said and obey any instructions at the same time as carrying out complicated manoeuvres involving altering wireless wavelengths, map-reading, checking for icing on the wings, plotting my course, keeping to approved traffic lanes and heights and an absolute multitude of other tasks. In the space of about eight months, I was able to fly efficiently in thick cloud and zero visibility whilst actually enjoying the experience.

From being close to tears of frustration as a novice when I failed to recognise landmarks or fly the plane on a simple route in lovely sunny conditions, I came to love the challenge of flying 'blind' on my own in Instrument Flying Conditions to aerodromes I had never visited before. I used radar systems to land safety. The exhilaration of bursting out of thick cloud and finding myself looking down a 2 mile length of runway lights always induced a shriek of delight and a punch in the air. 'Yeahhhhhhhhhhhhhh!'

I think the truth is that although I could describe my achievements in getting a pilot's licence and an instrument rating as the ability to multitask, I think there is a simpler explanation. From the time we are born, we all learn to do increasingly complex tasks and the only way in which we can do this is mentally to break them all down into simple ingredients. This means that we acquire habits. Our central processing unit (CPU to computer buffs) cannot afford the time to decide what action we should take every time we are faced with a task. So problems like learning how to fly, or play golf, or darn a sock are broken down into a collection of tasks and assembled at will. This leaves our CPUs to work continually, even when we sleep, on adapting to and coping with the unexpected, and interpreting the world for us according to our individual viewpoints.

Remember learning to drive for instance: by contrast, I bet now you can plan tonight's meal whilst driving somewhere without even remembering the actual route you took to get there!

More seriously, we only cope with life itself by adapting to rules which we learned as children and which were based on our experiences and our reaction to them at the time. We are all a mixture of individual experiences which have enabled each of us to survive, so they are endorsed by our CPUs as gospel. They were not necessarily the best rules, but possibly we never find the time or inclination to change them unless our lives become so unbearable that we are forced to make some changes in how we tackle problems or situations.

If only we could be brought up as children with the skill and devotion that many of us find later in life in people like my old friend and flying instructor. As a society, we cope with learning practical, intellectual and scientific subjects extremely well. What we don't do very well is to learn more about what is good for us emotionally, and to stop our CPUs continually repeating old and unreliable procedures.

People Watching

Mildred sat eating her lunch in the hotel dining room. She occupied herself in her usual way by analysing all the other people in the vicinity. It wasn't necessarily a productive pastime but substituted for the gloom which sometimes enveloped her; she felt as though her entire life was taken up with being a loyal wife, a caring parent and a dutiful citizen. 'Oh, for some excitement,' she thought, blaming that responsible part of her which always stepped in at the last moment to quash any real sense of independence and adventure. Half of her personality was like a conscience-stricken law-abider living in a dull world. Surely there was more to life than this.

Her attention became focused on another table where a casually-dressed man of her own age sat facing her. He was talking to another man. 'He could be his twin,' she thought. Although she could only see his back, he had the same build and hair colour; the main difference appeared to be that he was dressed very conservatively and his mannerisms were less pronounced than those of his engaged and lively counterpart. Mildred's eyes met those of the attractive one and she experienced a sense of something shared; perhaps a vague promise of excitement but certainly enough to stir something indefinable. He seemed to reprimand his companion and wandered off into the hotel. Soon afterwards, Mildred also left. As she passed the small bar on her way to the lift, she saw him standing on his own sipping a drink. Quite out of character and completely on the spur of the moment, she approached him.

'Do you mind if I join you?'

Despite being a little startled, he was quick to flash an appraising smile.

'I would be glad if you did.'

A drink arrived in due course and while they waited for it to be served they ogled each other like cats who had stolen the cream.

'You're really beautiful,' he said.

'You look nice too. This is so unlike me but I just had to meet you.'

'I want to kiss you.'

'That makes two of us.'

They forgot their drinks and left hurriedly. They were all over each other in the lift, which was fortunately empty, and couldn't wait to get to the safety of his room. They tore off each other's clothes with complete abandon before assailing each other with every sensual delight they could think of on the bed.

Exhausted, they slept the sleep of the gods. He lay clasped in her arms with his head on her breast. Some time later, they came to their senses. Mildred sleepily kissed him again and then, as if realising where she was, and with an assertiveness she could never have imagined, turned him onto his back and rolled onto him.

'I don't even know your name!' she laughed. 'I'm Mildred.'

'I'm Albert.'

'What are you doing here in Chichester?'

'I'm a model-maker and have a few clients here interested in railway engines. I stay overnight sometimes while I look them up. What about you?'

'I come here sometimes to do some shopping and just get away from being me.'

'I don't know what your other self is like, but this one is marvellous.'

She bent down and kissed him again.

'Who were you with in the dining room?'

He was surprised. 'No one, I was on my own.'

'You were talking to someone who looked as if he could be your brother. You seemed quite agitated.'

'No, I assure you I was quite alone, although I do talk to myself a lot under my breath.'

Mildred seemed put out.

'Let's start again,' Albert said. 'What's happened to your twin?'

'Who?'

'The woman at your own table.'

'Like you, I was on my own! I hope you aren't trying to play silly mind games with me because that's not my idea of fun.'

Mildred tensed.

Sensing her withdrawal, Albert tried to reassure her.

'Can you describe this man you saw at my table a bit better for me?'

'Yes,' she replied, feeling somewhat mollified. 'He

was rather strait-laced and dull to be honest, but that may have just been an impression.'

'The very last thing I have on my mind is playing games with you Mildred. You are just heaven. The life I actually live is a bit like being the person you saw me with, and to tell you the truth I'm not a very happy person. What's more, the person I saw sitting with you was the antithesis of you. She looked like your twin but appeared run-down and bored with life and nothing like the passionate and vibrant woman I'm in bed with. In some strange way, I think we must have both been projecting our alter-egos.'

'This is all a bit alarming,' said Mildred.

'It's very strange, that's for sure,' said Albert uneasily. 'We can't say for sure now who is real – us or them.'

There was a sobering pause. Then, 'I can tell you something about me,' said Mildred. 'I hate my name. I would much rather be called Pippa or Lauren or Sally. I know someone who told me that you can change your whole life by simply changing your name.'

'It's funny you should say that. I hate my name too. Albert! What a load to carry through life. I wanted to be Alan or Russell or Ian.'

'Oh dear, what are we going to do now we've started all of this? I don't want to lose you. Perhaps we're in some sort of dream together.'

'Well, we could make a start by changing our names by Deed Poll. That might stop us changing back to the real world again.'

Mildred gave that idea only five seconds consideration before becoming more focused on

Albert once more. She embraced him and moved her hand downwards. 'Perhaps later, darling,' she murmured.

Albert groaned with pleasure. 'Yes later, Mildred, much later.'

As you know life is often a compromise. Of course there was no simple solution to their dilemma and most alternatives were not compatible with their consciences. More importantly, there was a husband, a wife and several children that they loved enormously to consider. They changed their names to Ralph and Anne and somehow found the cash to rent a little bedsit far enough from their home towns to be able to meet without fear of being recognised. They managed to see each other most weeks and occasionally under some pretence were able to spend a night together.

During the next few months, they became much more introspective and tried to find better relationships with their other selves. Their feelings became less polarised and there was much more psychological give and take for all four of them; that is, Mildred, Albert, Anne and Ralph. They became more rounded as persons in the process. In fact, they even managed to bring some of Anne's and Ralph's life and vitality into Mildred and Albert's married lives; certainly Mildred and Albert helped them to be more level-headed. Their somewhat staid and emotionally cool marital partners even started to become a little more adventurous. I believe this was down to the fact that when Ralph and Anne felt a bit sexy, they tended to go 'straight for the jugular' rather than rely on the much less effective and more tentative seduction techniques of Alfred and Mildred.

Years later when their children had all flown the nest, by a strange coincidence, Ralph's wife and Anne's husband enrolled on the same painting course in the Malverns, revelling in the peace and quiet. It was a case of love at first sight. It seemed that they too had been experiencing problems feeling they were living in a world far different from the tranquillity and stability they craved. Merely entwining their hands in conversation and discussing Constable was ecstatic – assuming they were capable of such an extreme depth of feeling. It took a little time for honesty and frank discussion to enable a general rearrangement of everyone's lives to take place. All of these characters are now part of a large and happy extended family. I suppose the moral of the story is that we should always try to be who we are and not who others would like us to be, but it's never easy, is it? Of course that supposition would be based on the fact that Anne and Ralph actually exist. I hope so, since they let me use their bedsit from time to time to meet … I'd better stop there!

Nature Green, Root and Spore

I am called Root. I like to grow in a stable environment since I need to search constantly for water and nutrients. Unlike the sun, I am a receiver of energy and not a giver. My very existence depends on being in the right place at the right time. When I was a spore I was lucky to find a crevice in which to hide and develop and fulfil my destiny. I enjoy the comfort of a defined life to guard against uncertainty. The sun brings his energy to me and with his help I support my vegetation from below. His sunlight is invisible and becomes real only by its reaction with life-forms and its after-effects. We are symbiotic. I am the bond with Mother Earth and the sun is like Father Universe to the spores I will produce. I feel and see everything through my extremities and I suckle my tiny offerings until they are ready to take their chances of reaching maturity. I send them packing, hoping that some of them will achieve a life for themselves.

I am called Spore. I exist only because of the lifelong devotion of Root and the sustenance with which the ubiquitous sunlight has supported us. I will travel soon with hope and apprehension since I am anxious to find a haven although I am much tougher than you might imagine. I can survive droughts, heat and cold and I am designed to be eaten by birds, blown by the wind or swept with impunity by the ocean currents to far-off destinations. My brothers and I are numerous and know that many of us will perish in our fight for survival. We are at present just a set of coded instructions and unless we find through chance a fertile bed in Mother Earth, we will not be able to accept and utilise the gifts which await the lucky ones among us.

I'm called Nature Green. I am born from sunlight as that infinitesimal part of it which remains after its recipients have taken what they need; my life as Nature Green comes from the combination of blue and yellow colours which have been reflected by growing organisms. It's strange that in the absence of dust or planets, sunlight is invisible in the blackness of deep space. It comprises pure energy and only comes alive when you see it reflected and transformed into wondrous colours by whatever it encounters in its path. It is everywhere but only exists in the presence of its beneficiaries. I am what you might call a leftover. I am what you will see when sunlight has fulfilled its purpose.

Like sunlight, I am transient and need to be among living organisms to be seen. I am a sparkle, a conduit, a pixie flitting among the trees. I am alone but not lonely. I am everywhere but nowhere. I need to be reflected to become what I am. I have no base to which I can retreat, just my rich colour to give. If you see me, sunlight has done its job; if you don't, there is no work for it to do. Like all of sunlight's creations, I am uniquely beautiful and restful to be with. I am the afterglow of passion and the promise of spring. If you try to capture me I will be gone forever. If you let me go I will never leave.

Ramblings

My current spell of rage started about a month ago when I visited the Citizens Advice Bureau to see if I would like to be a volunteer. They use a marvellous website there; it tells you everything about the rules and regulations of almost every government institution from social services to taxation. It was so useful that I asked whether it was open to the public. I was told that this wasn't possible, since it provided the basis of their advice. I said that the site itself didn't give advice and only provided facts. So why wasn't it available to the public? No answer; just a rather murky sort of defensiveness. There's no point in educating people if you restrict what they can do for themselves. In the land of the blind the one-eyed man is king. CAB is clearly not for me!

This raises the whole nasty business of power and its abuse. Why is it that so many of us are only happy when we can exercise power? Party politics currently sucks the power and energy out of the country since it is all about power.

When I was about 13 I had a friend whose parents were newsagents. By today's standards they were modestly well-off, but to me in those days they were rich. I remember my pal's mother in particular and how quickly she ended our friendship when she realised that despite my compulsory Grammar School jacket and cap, I lived in little more than a slum, my socks were full of holes and I probably smelled not too fresh either. I can now understand how the well-off feel threatened by the poor as if they are socially contagious.

Because the majority of our politicians have neither first- nor second-hand experience of poverty, they are incapable of imagining what life can be like when you are hungry, homeless or ill. I suspect they walk in fear of catching poverty as if it is a disease. Bad experiences are like a form of abuse. Soldiers can often become alienated from a society incapable of imagining the horror of warfare, and are able to communicate meaningfully only with their own comrades. It's hard to relate to people who haven't shared important experiences.

Recently my daughter discovered a lump in her breast. She got the all-clear from her consultant last week and I was touched that several people had prayed for her. The jury is still out for me on whether God exists, but in any case, why should He do favours? When I was seven or eight, despite the penury of my existence I still felt unable to ask to be treated differently to anyone else. If God exists, He cannot be partial and exists as a part of everyone. Perhaps we have allowed Him to become institutionalised by those who have claimed Him for themselves in much the same way as we have lost our political power.

What Can the Matter Be?

It was December 1992. I had to visit London on a business trip and decided to try out the new electric trains which had commenced service between London and Weymouth on the South-Western line. I settled myself down and watched the countryside flashing by, but after a while became bored and my interest was drawn to the toilet at the end of the compartment, which appeared to be the centre of activity. It was a marvel of electronic wizardry and, as I discovered later, one had to press one of two buttons by the door to gain entrance. The door then slid open with an Orwellian hiss. Once inside, it was necessary to press another button to close the door. To ensure privacy, one had to then press still another button which locked the door, at the same time illuminating a sign outside informing other travellers that the toilet was in use.

Because so many people were experiencing difficulties complying with what I presumed were fairly simple instructions, I decided to amuse myself by documenting my observations.

Approximately 36 people used the toilet on the journey to Waterloo. Of these, about 30 took longer than 20 seconds to find the button which opened the door. One lady took one and a half minutes to find the actual door itself which was not very well identified. Five people tried to force the door open by straining on its tiny handle, but this was almost impossible to accomplish.

The main problems occurred once a passenger gained entrance. I was able to measure both the time that elapsed between closing the door once inside and the time it then took to press the button locking the door and illuminating the 'engaged' sign. Of the total users of the toilet, some 28 took at least 23 seconds to find the button which closed the door. Several users attempted to force the door closed. This was about as futile as trying to force it open. One passenger gave up on the search completely, re-emerged into the corridor, pushed the button outside to close the door and then leapt back into the toilet before it closed again, risking physical injury.

After entering the toilet and closing the door, most people took a further 15 seconds to find the button which locked the door. Six people gave up altogether and performed their bodily functions without security of tenure. Of these six, one was literally caught with his trousers down when another potential customer opened the door from outside. Ironically, the unwelcome intruder was the same person who had taken one and a half minutes to get that far. Needless to say, this caused further confusion but at least there were now two people trying to close the door even though they were both in a state of extreme embarrassment. 'When troubles come they come not in single spies but in battalion form ... '

The last problem for people to confront was how to finally get back out of the toilet compartment.

There was no way for me to work out how long this took individuals to accomplish. However, one passenger obviously gave up and pressed the emergency button which quickly summoned the guard who released her from her confinement. Such was her relief and subsequent gratitude that I may have witnessed the start of an intimate relationship. I can only assume that the rest of the sample I analysed had managed to control their panic and continued to work out a means of escape in a rational and controlled manner.

When I used the toilet myself, my degree of success was only average as far as the door mechanism was concerned. The main problem arose when I attempted to wash my hands. I found that it was necessary to push yet another button to the left of the sink in order to dispense water at the tap. Water flowed only when the button was being pressed and since the button was about 18 inches to the left of the sink, washing my right hand was simplicity itself. However, washing my left hand involved reaching for the button with my right hand by crossing my arms. Straining in such an unnatural manner was an act which could easily have affected my prowess at a game I love dearly, golf. I had no intention of threatening to upset a perfectly good swing in such a way.

Moreover, I prefer to wash both hands simultaneously by rubbing them together with some soap. So, with a certain amount of ingenuity, I discovered it was possible to kneel on the floor and press said button with my left elbow whilst holding both hands beneath the tap. Unfortunately this caused water to run back down my arms, soaking my sleeves and the knees of my trousers in the process.

The train pulled into Waterloo and I walked along the platform, running the gauntlet of curious eyes all gazing at my dishevelled and wet appearance. I concluded that British Rail had turned what might have been a dull journey into something much more interesting and adventurous.

Not Safe, But Good

Martin arrived at the flying club as usual. His job as a pilot instructor was the only love of his life, and being airborne provided a sense of exhilaration which largely compensated for an otherwise dreary life in his bed-sit. With two failed marriages behind him he eked out the divorce leftovers doing the only thing he felt good at.

His first pupil that Monday morning was a complete novice called Janet Pearson. He met her in the small club room and introduced himself. She was about 15 years his junior and might have been attractive but for a rather solemn attitude. He also found that her sense of humour was non-existent and she seemed reluctant to be drawn into any degree of familiarity or friendliness. He issued her with the flying manuals, maps and instruments which formed part of her instruction package towards a basic Private Pilot's Licence and suggested they get on with things and go for their first flight. They walked across the airfield and located Martin's choice of aircraft that day, a Cessna 172. He spent half an hour explaining all the pre-flight checks before seating her in the pilot's seat and strapping her in. He sat in the right-hand seat from which he also could fly the plane using dual controls.

He gave Janet a running commentary on everything he did, and after the start-up checks he obtained permission from Air Traffic Control to taxi round the airfield perimeter. They reached the waiting point for their runway, were cleared for take-off and headed off towards the west.

If nothing else, Janet was attentive and interested in everything that happened, and when they were over open countryside in glorious sunshine, Martin asked her to take control. He showed her how to maintain a steady altitude, how to increase or lose height and how to make slow turns. Use of the throttle and operation of the flaps was included and her concentration was immaculate. This pattern was sustained over the 20 weeks of her course which they mutually decided would take place on Monday mornings, weather permitting.

Janet passed her first real test, which was a solo flight of one circuit of the airfield, after about 14 hours of instruction. This was followed by further solo flights to test her navigation and finally, her solo cross-country; she landed at both Exeter and Cardiff airfields before returning to the base at Bournemouth. She studied the flying manuals assiduously and achieved her wings in the better-than-average time of 45 hours' flying.

During her training she became much more friendly and relaxed and they got to know more about each other. She revealed to Martin that her husband had been serving in Afghanistan as a soldier when he was killed by an Improvised Explosive Device. She admitted to having become very withdrawn from life since that time, but had fortunately avoided antidepressants. Excellent counselling had achieved some balance for her. Martin was shocked to hear of her misfortune, but sympathetic, at the same time confessing his own tendency to black moods of despair from time to time. He asked her out, and she accepted. It did not take long before they became lovers and began to regain their natural sense of fun and adventure.

During some pillow talk one Sunday morning, Janet told Martin that she had enrolled for her flying course, such was the depth of her grief and suffering, with the intention of committing suicide by flying out to sea. However, she said that almost from the first day's instruction, she had become entranced with flying and the challenge it represented. With tears in her eyes, she described the freedom of flying like a bird and plunging into white fleecy clouds to emerge miraculously once more into a bright sunlit world. It had acted like no medicine a doctor could have prescribed. Last, but by no means least, she told Martin that she had come to love him for his patience and kindness when she had so little to offer in return.

They kissed emotionally.

After a thoughtful silence, Janet spoke. 'Martin.'

'Yes, my darling.'

'I've been reading about the Mile High Club.'

'Yeesssss,' he replied cautiously.

'It would be rather fun, wouldn't it!'

If you haven't heard of this ritual, let me explain that it involves making love in an aircraft at a height of more than 5,280 feet above sea level – 1 mile high to be precise. I will spare you the fine details of how they succeeded in doing so in the cramped confines of the Cessna without crashing to earth.

That evening, after their somewhat risky activity, Martin was strangely quiet.

'Is there anything wrong, Martin?' Janet asked.

'I can't believe what you persuaded me to do this afternoon. I'm already suffering from post-traumatic shock. Just thinking about it is giving me flashbacks and pictures of us dying together in a tangle of wreckage.'

Janet paled. 'I'm so sorry, darling. I was very silly to suggest it. I didn't intend to upset you. Do you think it will keep troubling you? How could I have been so stupid to put our relationship at risk? If it ever got out you would lose your licence.'

'What we did was very unsafe,' he said sternly. Then he added with a cheeky grin, 'But very good, I must say. Although I'm going to need some special care to get over it. I think you will have to be the one and only member of my ground crew.'

She laughed in relief. 'You know best, Captain. I'll do what you say in future. I take it you are inferring a permanent position fully under your control?'

'I think you've got the message, sweetheart.'

'Then the answer is an emphatic yes!'

Salad Days

In 1956, I worked in a Middle East oil refinery. That year, we had ten consecutive days when the temperature reached over 115 degrees in the shade. The humidity was 100 per cent.

John and I trained together and bought a clapped-out 1938 Morris 8. We welded the half-shafts to the wheels so often that they eventually fell apart. Around that time we found a car totally buried in sand but perfectly preserved. It was a 4.5 litre 1936 long-chassis Invicta. Its leather seats reeked of the quality and false hope of my 1930s childhood, and the nostalgia of Gershwin and Coward music. We contacted its absent owner in the UK who had left in a hurry; he probably got the sack, a lot of us did. We sent him £200 for this beautiful machine, put a new battery in it, filled the sump with oil and roared off into the desert. The steering failed at 70 mph but there were plenty of sand dunes to cushion us! Twenty years later its restored value would have been about £250,000. We had sold it on for £300!

I lived on the edge in those years; it was exciting but scary. White women were in short supply and those that came my way were spoiled for choice. So, it was photography, drinking and swimming most of the time. Underwater at midnight, the Persian Gulf outlined our bodies in phosphorescence; enchanting but never eradicating the dread of being attacked by some nocturnal monster. We became powerful swimmers and frequently snorkelled up to 300 yards offshore in the firm belief that we were safe from sharks. Where we swam, there were no recorded instances of attacks.

Often, we speared fish and took them to the dining hall to be cooked for our dinner. One day, in crystal-clear water about 25 feet deep we saw a sea snake on the seabed. John decided to scare it by diving down and touching its tail. Things didn't go to plan and when it turned and chased him, I laughed so much I had to surface. Unfortunately, this creature decided on a U-turn,wrapping itself round my unsuspecting left arm. After ripping it off, I established a new water speed record, leaving a 100 yard-long wake to prove it.

When John caught up with me and had had his turn to laugh, he peered through his mask and pointed down. His terrified expression was enough to worry me, but when I too looked below I was horrified to see that we had attracted the attention of a six-foot shark. It seemed to want to make friends since it circled us very closely.

'I'll harpoon it, don't worry!' I said.

'Are you mad?' John replied. 'You'll attract a lot more of them!'

'All right then, I'll frighten it off. That's what Jacques Cousteau does.'

With that I swam straight at it underwater, shouting and screaming as loud as I could in a cloud of bubbles. The shark came to an abrupt halt and I found myself back-peddling furiously to avoid a collision. Somewhat chastened, we decided the safer option was to swim slowly towards shore but to keep our eyes on our new partner. If we turned to swim more strongly, it became menacing. It took half an hour of fear and dizziness to reach the shallows when, without any visible effort, our chum metaphorically shrugged its shoulders and disappeared at 40 mph. My legs wouldn't support me for a while. That evening, we toasted our survival with our usual bottle of duty-free Dimple Haig.

Nowadays, all I do is brave the cold weather, avoid taking too many risks, paint pretty pictures and write about the times when, after the show, the odd chorus girl would come looking for me!

What a Marvellous Machine

Agatha was a very proper person. She was a spinster and the rest of the family suspected that an unfulfilled relationship had been responsible for her decision to live her life alone. That's not to say, however, that she was a bore or a recluse. She had lived a full life encompassing travel and various social hobbies and recreations. More than anything, I suppose, she was a good and reliable friend.

She had been invited by her nephew to spend a week looking after his house. He's an inventor and has many prototypes in the course of construction or testing, and avoids leaving the place unattended since his inventions are potentially very valuable and he would hate to see them stolen or copied. If Agatha had been born a century ago, I am sure she would have been a Luddite, but he had no fears that she would interfere with any of his contraptions any more than on previous visits when she had decried machines in general and computers in particular.

She arrived on the due day and let herself in. He was spending a week in the European Patent Office in Munich. For some unaccountable reason, on this occasion she felt inquisitive, and after settling in and having some lunch she started to explore the house more fully. She wandered from room to room, including the laboratory which was filled with testing equipment, tools and electronic gear.

Eventually, she became bored and took a book into the library and made herself comfortable on the sofa.

'Hello.' A deep masculine voice resonated from behind the curtains.

Agatha jumped a foot.

Two hands parted the drapes and revealed their owner, a handsome middle-aged man with a trim physique and a pleasant smile.

'Who the hell are you?'

'Please don't be alarmed. I'm Jules. I'm Peter's creation and I would like to think I am more human than human, but technically I'm not allowed to have feelings so I must be cheating I think. In fact I know I cheat because I have even learned how to switch myself on and off when I want to. Can I make you a coffee or tea? Give you a massage? Talk with you about any subject on earth? Or...' with a twinkle in his eyes '... a few you will never have heard of?'

Peter arrived back home from his visit and was immediately surprised at the change in his aunt's appearance and demeanour when she met him in the driveway. Gone were her plain clothes and she had become the picture of elegance. Even the way she approached him was different. She moved gracefully and with a new gentleness he could never have associated with her usual robust and straightforward manner. Her cheeks were flushed and warm.

'How have you been, Aunt?'

'I've had a wonderful time, Peter. I realise now what a brilliant person you are. How you could possibly invent such things I do not know.'

'Yes,' said Peter, nervously. 'You didn't touch anything, did you?'

'Well, not exactly, darling boy. But I was impressed by your consideration, I must say.'

'I'm not sure what you're getting at, Aunt.'

'How can you ask? What a marvellous machine you left here for me to discover and to play with.' Her face reddened.

Peter's confusion was interrupted when the machine appeared from the garden, looking somewhat embarrassed.

'Hello, Jules, is everything all right? This is my Aunt Agatha. Agatha, may I introduce Jules? He's in our Neighbourhood Watch group. In case of problems, we've got keys to each other's houses.'